Odyssey of Innocents

Also by Lydia Edwards

The Truckee River Experience

Odyssey
of
Innocents

A Harrowing Journey Westward to Freedom

For Mary Ann —
"We found our
path by walking"
Thank you for
the path we've
traveled together,
and the journey
never ends!
love always,
Lydia

Lydia Edwards

ARCHWAY
PUBLISHING

Archway Publishing books may be ordered through booksellers or by contacting:

Archway Publishing
1663 Liberty Drive
Bloomington, IN 47403
www.archwaypublishing.com
1 (888) 242-5904

ISBN: 978-1-4808-1684-8 (sc)
ISBN: 978-1-4808-1682-4 (hc)
ISBN: 978-1-4808-1683-1 (e)

Library of Congress Control Number: 2015905542

Print information available on the last page.

Archway Publishing rev. date: 04/21/2015

For my brother, Richard.

The west shall shake the east awake.
Walk while ye have the night for morn.
—James Joyce, *Finnegans Wake*

Contents

Introduction

The Arab Spring was the revolutionary wave of demonstrations and protests (both non-violent and violent), riots, and civil wars in the Arab world that began in December 2010. Five years earlier, as a result of the invasion of Iraq, the seeds lying dormant then suddenly burst forth in the tiny nation of Tunisia on the Mediterranean coast. Democratic uprisings arose independently and spread quickly to Egypt, Libya, Syria, Lebanon, Yemen, Bahrain, Saudi Arabia, and Jordan.

On December 18, 2010, the Tunisian Revolution began when Mohammed Bouazizi, a twenty-six-year-old street vendor, was refused a street license to sell his goods, and police confiscated his cart and beat him because he didn't have a permit. When he went to the municipal office to file a complaint, the workers ignored him. In desperation, Bouazizi set himself on fire. He died nine days later.

Small-scale demonstration then spread throughout the country. Bouazizi's act of despair highlights the public's boiling frustrations over living standards, police violence, rampant unemployment, and a lack of human rights.

Within four short months, in March 2011, smoldering unrest from political corruption reached Syria. The conflict turned into an anti-government uprising, followed by three years of war and the threat of US air strikes, nearly destroying this Middle Eastern nation. But President Bashar al-Assad's government fought its way back with a relentless military campaign of air strikes, shellings, and strategic use of siege warfare on insurgent-held areas, which turned into bloody massacres and deadly chemical bombings.

The full-blown civil war has killed more than one hundred ninety thousand, displaced nine million Syrians, and destroyed 60 percent of the industry and 40 percent of the houses. Syrian refugees continue to flood neighboring Lebanon, Jordan, Iraq, and Turkey. Millions of civilians are traumatized in the displaced chaos of refugee camps and suffer disease epidemics, starvation, and death.

International aid agencies report that every statistic tracking the lives of Syrian children has worsened as the conflict grinds on and warns that an entire generation is at risk. UNICEF estimated last year that 2.3 million children were in need of shelter, food, health care, education, or psychological help for the trauma they suffered. That number has doubled to 5.5 million children in 2014.

The calamity in Syria is getting worse! Radical militant armies continue to threaten the Middle East, and terrorism is spreading globally. The numbers are staggering—thousands murdered, and more have fled. In terms of refugees, changing lives, or saving children, the impact is unknown.

Brutal militant separatists have spread terror throughout Iraq and Syria, uprooting more families.

A new generation of refugees is cast. Will this be the children's awakening? Has the odyssey of innocents begun?

Author's Note

This is a work of fiction; however, I have woven my personal family relationships and conceptualized them into today's current crisis in the Middle East. While global nations continue on their same madness of oppression and aggression, with worldwide suffering and without regard to human rights, my abhorrent distaste for war is apparent. I've injected critical forethought that demands thorough reconsideration of our policies and beliefs.

To cite John Lennon's poetic and noble anthem ... yes, John, *we can* "Imagine."

MAP I – NEAR EAST – THE LEVANT
SYRIA, LEBANON, ISRAEL, WESTBANK-PALESTINE

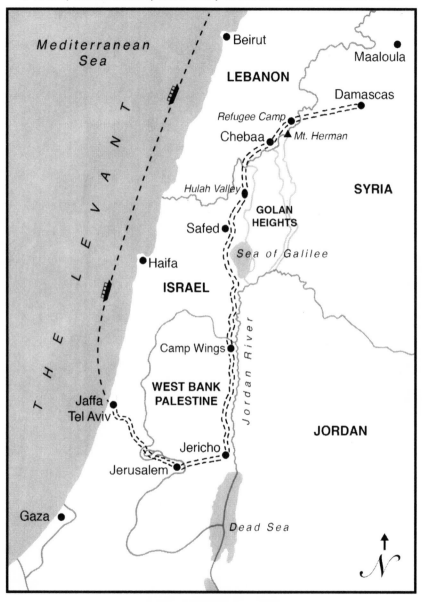

10   20   30   40   50
MILES

Part One

Follow the Sun

Prologue

Damascus, Syria

Late spring 2013

"God is not Allah. God is love," my mother, Rama, whispered. She pulled the blanket, warm and secure, around my shoulders with the tightest tuck and tug of the sheets. In her mysterious and gentle wisdom, she added, "Do not tell your father this. He will only scold you, Tania. He doesn't see clearly sometimes. Love is what I know. It is what I feel for you and your brothers and your sister. Love keeps me alive, not Allah." She gave me a quick sweet kiss.

Suddenly the evening sky flashed with unnatural brilliance. A violent explosion from the streets below—all too familiar now—sent shock waves through our two-story building.

"Hush," Mother whispered. "There could be another one."

We waited, not moving. The wailing of sirens filled the silence.

I

Exodus from Damascus
Summer 2013

A violent civil war in Syria that began in January 2012 has thrown the nation into chaos, ravaged by atrocities and the horrors of a ruthless regime. The besieged people of Damascus were forced to flee for the borders of Lebanon and Jordon, where refugee camps are strung along the western and southern boundaries.

We, the Abu Ali family, and our relatives quickly gathered what we could carry. We packed dry goods and water stocked from our once-successful restaurant located below our modern two-story apartment. We brought sustainable vegetables and fruit—potatoes, squash, apples, and melons—two pots, long spoons, and spices. We carried bed rolls of rugs, blankets, and only essential clothing strapped to our backs. The many children, young and able like ourselves, resembling pack mules, were laden with backpacks and bottles of water. The future unknown, our precious cell phones were the first to be packed.

My father, Khaled, and mother, Rama, had four children: my sister, Jadeen, fifteen; my brother, Fareed, fourteen; me (Tania), thirteen; and the youngest brother, Davi, ten. My mother's sister, Sonia, and her husband, Rashad Saada, joined the family exodus. From a once-thriving suburb of Damascus, we joined masses of refugees as most trudged for three days to safety to Lebanon.

Fortunately, my father was able to flag down one of the private vans that scouted the road for those willing to pay the price for a ride to the border, sparing us the grueling passage.

We arrived at the Lebanese refugee camp that resembled a massive campout among the throng of homeless. We were assigned and registered to our new dwelling, among long rows of military square-tent housing made of polymer-foam panels supported by flexible steel frames. Once inside, the blunt odor of plastic altered the sweet smell of incense coming from our belongings. Despite this we preferred the kinder demons of stifling heat than the unbearable choking dust devils that swirled outside.

Evenings came as a blessing because this was when calm prevailed. Aromas of onions and garlic wafted throughout the camp.

Humanitarian centers provided a line of electricity to each tent for portable electric cook tops. Clean water and food was distributed for the neediest, but as more refugees flooded the camp, the sanitation and washing centers were strained to keep up. The women filled the centers day and night with laundry duties.

Late that night, thinking the washing centers would be less crowded, Jadeen and I approached a long line of women, some to the bathroom, others to wash.

As we left, I said, "This is going to be a living hell."

"Yeah," Jadeen said, disgusted. "This is no magic carpet ride."

———•◦•———

Rumors had been spreading of attacks against us from our own Assad government. Insurgents were beginning to counterattack. Syria was worldwide news.

It had only been two days, but the stress was palpable. Even the two brothers, Fareed and Davi, who were gone most of the time investigating their newly found environment, grew less animated around the adults.

My father, becoming more incensed by the news, spoke quietly to Uncle Rashad about returning to

Damascus and joining the Free Syrian Army's rebel opposition against the Assad regime. They devised a plan as not to alarm the women and children. They agreed this would soften their intent of returning to Damascus.

How they hated to be driven and displaced by their own government. They became rabid in their convictions, feeding on each others' bitterness and thirst for revenge.

"That little rat of a tyrant's days are numbered," Rashad pledged. "I want to be there to storm his palace, to see him dead the way he has murdered us."

———————

Like most Muslims, both had been raised in the traditional Islamic beliefs requiring men to serve in the military at age eighteen. Their culture encouraged brotherhood, which entailed long hours together. Male bonding was absolute! They prayed on their knees in unison, chanting in protest and demonstrating en masse. Even so, their primary bonding occurred in intimate circles while sipping fruit tea as they "ironed the heads" of kindred brothers, endlessly expounding on personal opinions until interrupted by another who took his turn with robust and swaggering chatter! When the discourse turned to the mass murders in Syria and aroused anger, someone would relieve the frustration, slap his knee, laugh, and recount the old myth "and there are seventy-two virgins waiting for brave martyrs in heaven."

My father wasn't very domineering but displayed proud, unrestrained vigor. He filled a room with his humor and presence. He was gentle and patient with us, filling our needs, mainly our stomachs. He was the best cook who could make in a single pot a lamb stew with peppers, onions, and beets that tasted like a feast. It delighted our senses and nourished us for an entire day. However, he had a temper that could shock us into silent angst.

After a few days, he became agitated and restless. Cooking lentil beans and lamb stew at noon in the tent had become unbearable. I noticed he and my uncle would slip away and huddle with the surrounding men.

One night everything erupted! I had never seen my parents argue or raise their voices to one another, let alone what happened that night.

"Rashad and I are going back to our country—not to join the rebels like many men here but to save our restaurant and our home," Father announced to Mama.

My mother, the story of her life reflected in soft, iridescent hazel eyes, had become weary and exhausted and depended more than ever on her sharp-edged independent sister. Aunt Sonia motioned us to remain silent. Expectant and fearful, we watched the drama unfold among our family.

Shocked, Mother pleaded, "But you cannot go. Your family ..."

"You and Sonia can care for them, but we are taking Fareed with us," Father insisted.

The heavy air became toxic in our tiny tent. Mama looked pleadingly about her. Sonia remained silent. The children, stricken, were huddled in a corner, eyes wide with apprehension.

Mama stiffened. "You go, but Fareed stays here. I forbid you take a boy into that—"

"You defy me?" Father's eyes strained with anger.

Mama, fearless and unashamed, answered with a hiss. "Yes."

A bitter family quarrel broke out, the men insisting my older brother, Fareed, join them in going back to Damascus.

Fareed stood in opposition. "I won't go, Papa. To leave them here would be dishonorable."

Enraged, Father shouted at Mama, "See what you have done?"

My mother, encumbered by her robes, spun away, reeled backward, and fell. She landed, dazed, on the ground, her robe and head scarf resembling unfolded laundry.

Sonia quickly pulled open the door flap of the tent. In defiance she gestured for the men to leave.

Khaled and Rashad gathered their belongings and diverted their eyes from the silent and horrified group around them. The men exited without looking back, rebellious and unable to mask their male pride.

My bewilderment quickly turned to anger. I dare not speak but vowed, *I don't care to ever see them again.*

Alone now, Sonia comforted Mother, shaken and bruised. Then she attempted to stand, but fell backward, moaning "It's my ankle."

Sonia, still kneeling, whispered to her sister, "The children must go—it's dangerous here—food is scarce. Together they can help each other—the older ones are competent and smart."

Mama uttered, "Tell them where to go—to Jerusalem."

Sonia replied, "I know." She skillfully assured us children she would care for our mother. "You must leave together, the four of you—to a safer place." She paused, letting this news sink in. "And remember this"—Sonia, a woman wise in the ways of nature, continued—"go west in search of the great sea called the Mediterranean."

"Why?" I wondered aloud.

"Because, Tania, we come from the sea—it's our source. Do our tears not taste of salt? Can the palm exist in a desert of sand without water?"

Aunt Sonia, the invariable teacher, educated in Jerusalem where she taught English and history, frequently traveled back to her roots in Damascus, where she met and married Rashad, an ambitious real-estate advisor. Sonia continued teaching at the Syrian Private University until the civil war changed and ravaged their lives.

Undaunted, Sonia never let an opportunity pass without a lesson. Her teacher instincts took over. She looked every bit as fierce as a tiger with her short, permed hair she had liberated years ago when she discarded the traditional hijab. As the firm, clear words erupted from her mouth, we were held captivated by her instructions.

"Remember; go west—you can follow the sun. Our ancestors would have. When the sun sets at night, draw a circle in the sand with an arrow pointing where the sun sets, which is always in the west. Follow the arrow! Do not be confused when you awaken at dawn when the sun is rising in the east at your back, for it will change at high noon, right above you. Then follow the sun, always keeping it in your face. Make sure your shadow is then behind you. The sun will lead you west."

I hope the other kids are getting this, I thought.

"If you must detour, go south. Find the Jordan River and follow it to Jericho. Then head west to Jerusalem, where I have friends. Go to the Hebrew University of Jerusalem and find Anna Gold. She will tell you how to reach my friends. Rama and I will meet you there as soon as we are able. Anna Gold will be our contact.

"You don't have passports, so tell the border guards you became separated from your parents. Make up a story that meets your needs at the time.

"Now stay together! And watch out for one another. You are wiser than most children your age; I've watched you grow. Double up on your clothes and wear them, don't carry them.

"Girls, change into jeans, braid your hair, and tuck it under your cap. Trust women! Women sympathize with children. Stay away from groups of beggars. They are orphans, but you are not.

"Take your cell phones—hide them and don't lose them! Use my account, I'll try to extend it. Charge your phones when you can."

"Better to sleep in the darkness than in large villages. It is still warm, thank goodness! War is all around us, in the towns and cities. Jerusalem isn't far, but there will be obstacles. Overcome them! Do not separate—always stay together! Now sleep."

———•·•———

Sleep? How could I sleep? Rapid and jolting images sped across my mind—Mama's anguish … my father's rage.

Yet gratefully, by means of Aunt Sonia's strength and guidance, she directed our liberation from this dreadful place—the thought of leaving would be another "romp-about" of discovery with my brothers and sister. We had already been a gang of four back in Damascus, where we were inseparable. Because we were so close in age, our shared dependence upon each other enabled us to sacrifice, be curious and bold, dare to take risks, learn from mistakes, and curiously observe the older folks' mysterious ways—their rigid and complicated actions.

As I lay there, I thought about life back in Damascus: our summers and long holidays that granted us the pure joy of living unhindered by adult supervision.

Our parents worked most of the day and evenings at our neighborhood restaurant, a popular gathering place for artists, musicians, and actors that attracted tourists seeking refuge from the clamoring metropolis of Damascus. In the mornings we would clean tables, sweep floors, and help prepare food. We seldom had a meal around a family table, but we never went hungry.

The scent of food lingered on our street. The warm, cheese-filled pastries dripping with sugary syrup and the best falafel and pizza rounds that came in ten varieties cast tantalizing scents from a block away.

Here we played soccer in the alleys, and men pushed around wooden carts selling melons. We'd hear the coos of pigeons, the rings of bicycle bells, and the stereo-projected voices calling the devout to prayer punctuated by the sounds of honking horns and revving of motorcycles.

When we felt adventurous, we'd catch the minibuses that traversed our larger playground—Damascus, praised as the Arab capital of culture. We'd join the international visitors who would lead the way off the bus, knowledgeable and prepared for their next important stop beyond which were universities, galleries, massive mosques, and undersized churches. Non-Muslim tourists always took particular interest in the walled Old City of Damascus, where St. Thomas's gate led to the Christian district of *Bab Tuma*.

Once we rambled through a museum where Jadeen took offense by the moral distaste of synthetic displays of staged ancient bloodthirsty battles, glorified victories, and bejeweled reigning kings. Gradually we lost interest and vowed never to return to old museums, seeking instead the grander brilliance of downtown Damascus. And when daylight lingered late during summer evenings, we'd spend hours at the enormous sports center watching field games or basketball games, and then move on to compete in our own raucous games of table tennis. We discovered a park nearby that provided rented horses on which we'd ride the trails, and if we remembered to bring our suits, we'd go swimming.

Returning home, our restaurant lighted and alive with customers, welcomed four enthusiastic but hungry kids. Those were blissful times. That was more than a year ago, before the civil war—

Syria, a liberal, multi-sectarian country with a progressive government, permitted and even encouraged girls to get an education—unlike stricter Middle Eastern Islamic regions.

We started school at age six. First Jadeen began, and then the rest of us followed. Although our lessons were academic, much of our learning came from interactions with customers who visited our restaurant from all around the world. Tourists inspired my parents to purchase a television similar to the one we have in our apartment, which provided CNN closed-captioned. And with the help of Aunt Sonia—The Professor, we called her—we became functional in many languages and dialects, especially Hebrew and English. She encouraged us to speak and read English. Her books of world cultures and religions were more compelling than the technology, business, and science that predominated Damascus education. Our aunt didn't hold back from her worldly knowledge—she was a captivating force, our surrogate professor right here in our own home. And we were her adopted and willing students—the children of her own she never had.

Fareed and I were sandwiched between Jadeen and Davi. We were all tall for our age with long arms and legs—all elbows and knees! My body was long and straight, and I wondered if I would ever have curves and a waist.

Fareed was the peacekeeper when we quarreled, and a cautious leader. He was handsome and gentle yet strong when our paths met danger. Fareed had a special magnetism about him; not one to brag, he was nonetheless confident, tolerant, and even noble. His infectious little chuckle, almost a giggle, concealed embarrassment and modest pride. How could a sister not admire a brother like that?

Jadeen, my older sister, was lithe, winsome, and had a stubborn streak. There was something unearthly about her, like maybe she came from another star that held secrets she dare not tell. She could dance and outrun us all and never boasted about it. I remember once when I saw a photo of the Three Graces (Joy, Charm, and Beauty)—that was Jadeen, but she had longer legs.

Davi, the youngest, was most fearless, probably because a ten-year-old boy had become emboldened by three older siblings. Davi looked upon our leaving the camp as a great adventure into the unknown. Because of his youth, he would have to be the one most guarded, although he didn't think so!

I trembled; a chilling shiver shook me from the wistful yearnings of days past. Now we must go into the unknown.

What brought us to this miserable refugee camp? Syrians killing Syrians! Rebels! Terrorists! A civil war they call it, but it doesn't sound civil to me. Why would my father and uncle leave like they did? To save our house and restaurant? Aren't we more important than a house? How could he have treated my mother like that?

I would never understand.

II

On Our Own

By a single light bulb, we packed our belongings. When it was my turn to say goodbye to Aunt Sonia and Mama, I kneeled and whispered, "I love you, Mama." Then I tucked the blanket gently about her shoulders.

We left at daybreak, the sun's glow just breaking, clearly at our backs. We headed out of camp packed with food stuffed in a backpack, a rug and afghan blanket bedroll, and some money. No one was at all curious that four kids among many were stirring in the morning. Slipping away from the refugee camp into the shadows and darkness, we found ourselves suddenly alone, strangers in a strange land, partly fearful but mostly excited and exhilarated.

Davi took it upon himself to explore his newfound freedom, discovering new terrain from our trail that led between massive rock formations. We laughed and agreed to put a leash on Davi, lest he got lost or worn out. The trees were becoming numerous and taller. We followed a path that led high up a mountain. It was becoming another escapade of curiosity and an uncertain tomorrow.

That night after a full day of travel, among the sanctuary of boulders on which we etched our westward circle and arrow, we settled in for our first evening completely alone. We felt grateful to be away from the squalor of refugees and the sand and dust.

"We need a plan, a story," Fareed decided. "A story of why we're traveling alone."

I agreed. "We can say we became separated from our parents, who went ahead of us."

Jadeen asked, "Okay, where were our parents going?"

"To Jerusalem," I said.

"All right, we agree; they are going to Jerusalem—to meet Anna Gold at the Hebrew University."

Davi was already asleep.

———•◦•———

The next morning we continued the steep trail upward, but we were excited to have the sun in our faces as we headed west. Gratefully, the path took a sharp curve south, away from the rugged path to the top of Mt. Herman.

Davi was the first to spot, or rather hear, the waterfall. He impulsively ran ahead and then raced back with the news. "A waterfall! It's awesome, and it's big, with a pool at the bottom."

Energized, we followed, and sure enough, there was a vertical cascade sliding down a gash in the mountains, spilling over a cliff into a wondrous pool of water. We stripped down to our underclothes and waded into the icy water, thankful to rid ourselves of the dirt. I exchanged glances of relief with my siblings while scooping up handfuls of water, drinking the purist, coldest water we never knew existed. We lingered by the pool for hours, letting the warm sun dry us. I'd forgotten how comforting it is to be with just my brothers and sister—no adults, no crowds, no upheaval in our lives. Once again we were exploring the wonders of the world around us. I was free, in the wild, one with nature again. It reminded me of our uninhibited evenings back home.

To no one in particular, I reminisced aloud. "Remember, back in Damascus we invented contest games at night when Mama and Papa worked late?"

We would turn off the lights, and in the darkness each of us would mimic a statue of imps and goblins, the more grotesque and outlandish the better.

Jadeen said, "When we were ready we'd shout 'turn on the light' and laugh—no, I mean convulse with laughter."

Fareed said, "And voted on the champion, the most comical and original pose would win. It was very competitive."

"Then we'd do it again and again." Jadeen laughed.

"Would you do it now?" I said.

Fareed shook his head. "No, we were just kids."

"What are we now?" Davi asked.

"Growing older by the day," Fareed said solemnly. His words sliced our memories into silence, exposing the reality of our journey as well as our bodies.

Time to get dressed.

———•◦•———

After the sun was clearly at our faces, Davi announced, "I'm hungry."

In a couple of hours we reached the village named Chebaa and came upon a structure resembling a mosque, with fig trees inside a garden. The ripe figs were irresistible. While we were picking and eating at the same time, never noticing a kindly gentleman, the servant of the mosque, approached us.

"No need to steal food, my children, this is a temple of worship, not a deli. Come inside. I have more."

After we filled our stomachs with bread and lentil soup, he enquired of our plans.

"To the Great Sea to the west," Fareed said.

"No, my children, there has been a terrible massacre along the coast. The West Bank is less dangerous than Lebanon right now. You must go south and stay on the main road to the highway to Galilee."

We thanked him and moved on. Forced to change direction, we trudged southward. Small encampments of villagers directed our way toward the Jordon River.

———•◦•———

Our first encounter with soldiers came suddenly when border guards at an Israeli checkpoint held their guns raised and eyed us suspiciously.

"Where are you going?" a guard demanded. "Show your passports."

Fareed stepped forward. "We're going west, to the Great Sea." Then he remembered "the story." "Our parents have our passports. We were separated at the refugee camp—we're to meet them in Jerusalem, where we have friends," he said flawlessly.

The guard laughed. "Heading west? Ha! Better you go south to Golan Heights, less gunfire and explosions. We have a war here; no place for babies."

Davi shouted, "I'm no baby!"

The guards then moved ahead to search each of us. Suddenly I remembered Mama's words, "God is love." I kept repeating them out loud as a chant.

The border guards stepped back a bit, as if I was bewitched. Satisfied with their search, they displayed their usual arrogant superiority, unaffected by the line of traffic that waited their inspections.

Taking advantage of the moment, Davi saw a lone woman in a car—and then with youthful exuberance he asked her for a ride!

Without hesitation, she graciously drove us for miles through the beautiful Huleh Valley west of the Golan Heights, where she dropped us off before turning west to Safed. "It's only a few miles to Galilee—maybe you will get lucky again for a lift, if you send your brother first." She laughed, waved, and drove off.

A small village near the highway attracted us. Wary at first, we curiously approached a bustling intersection, when Davi pointed to a gathering of families amongst a farmers' market.

He yelled excitedly, "Let's go see!"

"Let's not and say we did," Fareed said cautiously.

Davi argued, "Let's do it and say we didn't."

Fareed warned, "Davi, stay together."

Davi, always the first to run ahead toward the excitement, dashed into the market. Seconds later a bomb exploded. Davi was among the innocent victims.

Perhaps it was the concussion that killed him. Maybe we will never know; it all happened so fast.

Deafened by the blast, only my eyes revealed the horror rising from the dust and wreckage littered with vegetables and bodies.

I looked at Davi just before they covered his body …

I stood there; frozen, strong hands gripped my shoulders pulled me away. I pleaded but couldn't hear my words, "He's my brother! We can't leave him!"

With anguish on their faces, Jadeen and Fareed coaxed me into a car. I don't remember much of what happened next, but a few hours later we discovered each other gathered in the sanctuary of a synagogue. The rabbi gently offered words of solace—meaningless to me; I was still suspended in disbelief. He mercifully assured us that Davi would be buried with others from the tragedy in the graveyard with an engraved headstone.

Our lives changed forever that day.

———•·•———

We didn't know then that the sudden death of a loved one traumatizes instantly but fades in time. It unknowingly seeps and germinates within the psyche. It lives just beneath the surface, that searing, unforgiving, vivid horror.

Still in shock, my thoughts drifted as fatigue set in.

I want to sleep. I want to forget, forget the image of Davi. I wonder if Fareed and Jadeen are begging for sleep too. I can't comprehend the final truth, this bitter knowledge; like the sun, it blinds. I felt a hunger to escape, anything to replace the present—to sleep, find peace—but that acid-etched moment returned again and again in my memory.

We lost Davi.

We lost our innocence.

We found reality.

The Rabbi's Words

Distressed and spent, sleep mercifully came. When aroused by the rabbi, the horror of yesterday slowly began once again. We didn't belong here, and I begged my sister and brother to leave this place of destruction and death.

The rabbi, with grace and understanding, consoled us. "Look ahead, not backward, and continue to seek your mission to Jerusalem where friends will take kindly of your quest—be honest with them. You must believe; the goodwill of many will overcome malice of the deranged and unfortunate few." He firmly counseled, "Look forward; the past will soften, but for now you must look forward."

His simple words became a pledge and then my mantra. *Look forward, look forward*, I kept repeating.

Thus began our journey—a quest for truth-seeking, where life and death become as one, closer to earth than in faraway make-believe heavens. We had to keep moving or perish.

Everything looked different. Despite the radiant sunshine, the world around me was indistinct, as if I were peering into a pond, when reflecting beams of light slanted the image out of focus. Things of little value appeared tedious, even trivial.

———•◦•———

We left the village absorbed in the changing landscape the natural world unveiled. The horizon further away now, it became expansive when suddenly before us another splendid valley stretched out beyond. Farmland, perhaps once a lake, beckoned us like the migrating birds that followed the wetlands trail leading southward.

I remembered Aunt Sonia's words. "Follow the birds and find water."

III

Sea of Galilee

Israeli settlements and resort towns flourished along the shore of the life-giving waters of the Jordan River. The men glanced at us, but the women offered food and hurriedly sent us along our way.

The river flowed from a grand peaceful body of water. Could this be from the Great Sea we had been seeking?

From the highway, we followed a road leading toward the river that opened to a spacious park and campground densely shaded with palm and olive trees. A wide path of intricately laid stonework led us to the water's edge, where intimate groups of people assembled along the shore. Fascinated by a ceremony, we stopped to witness three people as they waded waist deep into the river and engaged in a ritual as their companions stood solemnly silent.

In the distance, I heard the high-pitched sounds of a flute drifting through the early evening. The soulful strains of the woodwind made me feel guilty and depressed. I felt like crying but became angry instead. I dared not look at Jadeen and Fareed, for their faces would remind me of what we had lost.

———•—•———

When the ritual was over, I asked a woman nearby, a tourist perhaps, wearing red knee-length shorts that matched a sun visor and red walking shoes. "Is this the Great Sea? Are we near Jerusalem?"

"No, no, not Jerusalem." She laughed. "This is the great sea of Lake Tiberius."

"But you said a lake."

"Yes, but really it's the Sea of Galilee. It's where we baptize the faithful."

Jadeen asked, "Who gets to be baptized?"

The woman proudly answered, "All who believe. Even Jesus was here … now Muslims, Jews, and Christians seek these waters."

"And they don't kill each other?" I blurted. *Perhaps these people can be trusted*, I thought. *Muslims, Jews, and Christians all in the same water? How strange …*

A small gathering formed. More questions. "Where are you from? Where are you going? Where are your mother and father?"

We were seduced by their kindness and compassion. Slowly we revealed our story. With sympathetic gestures, some gathered food in bags and offered clothes and shoes.

A woman and man approached us. "My name is Hannah, and this is my husband, Morel. Please rest with us tonight. We live close to the border of Lebanon and came here to escape the suicide bombings and shelling. Our camp is right over there." She pointed to the campground. "We'll have a campfire, plenty for dinner, and we have a story for you of Jesus."

Hannah, a petite, pretty woman, and Morel, a large, quiet man, took delight in showing off their cooking and camping skills.

Do they feel sorry for us—or is their kindness genuine? I wondered.

Fareed and Jadeen willingly accepted their hospitality. They made themselves comfortable after an enormous dinner.

We gathered our blankets about us and sat cross-legged near a campfire while Hannah revealed her story of Jesus while Morel cleared and cleaned the picnic table.

"Lake Tiberius, once known as the Sea of Galilee, is a very sacred place. For years it has been visited by pilgrims of many countries. They come here to be baptized, pay homage, pray, and receive blessings from the sweet waters of Galilee. It was here when Jesus was baptized by a holy man, John the Baptist, that he began his ministry of compassion and forgiveness."

My anger rose again. The more she spoke of Jesus, love, and peace, the more I wondered if Davi had ever been baptized. Would it have kept him alive? My attention wandered, and I was struck with the reality of the past days and how far the world around us had strayed from those messages.

Old wars, new wars, border wars, old religions, new religions—and all those churches! Is that what it's all about? Are we just going to be a line in the history books? What about just now? I was confused and didn't understand it all.

I slept the night in a stupefied trance—dreams transported me to a faraway land of bodies and babies, slowly raising high above me.

I woke with Fareed and Jadeen still asleep. I suddenly ached for my mother, a painful sorrow so deep I couldn't weep.

———•◦•———

Hannah, who symbolized all that Jesus portrayed, was the first to appear from her tent in the morning. She spoke softly. "Is everybody awake?"

No one stirred until she mentioned breakfast. My melancholy turned to gratitude when Morel prepared poached eggs atop pan-fried potatoes and peppers, hot pita bread, and coffee. He brushed aside our thanks, blushing. "Honored to be of service to you three, a hardy breakfast for a long journey ahead."

"Before you begin your journey down the Jordan River," Hannah explained, "you have a few miles before you reach the Jerusalem. And I must warn you, boys can pass through difficult situations where girls are not allowed. Rid yourselves of caps and head scarves and cut your hair short. Be wary of everyone, especially men. Not all men are as Morel." She turned, smiling at Morel.

I didn't know what Jadeen was thinking, but I thought it was a great idea. I asked Hannah to cut my hair and she did a pretty good job.

"I'm *not* going to cut my hair!" Jadeen blurted emphatically.

I didn't blame her. Her hair was long and thick with a slight wave that I envied. Mine was straight and fine. My short hair was a marked improvement.

I looked at Jadeen for approval. "I like my hair; don't you like it?"

"Go ahead, be a boy."

"Better than skirts too."

But Jadeen refused. She was having none of that. She had made up her mind and told Hannah, "I'll take my chances," as she pulled her head scarf and tied it into place.

That settled, Hannah advised, "If you travel quickly, you will reach the West Bank in two days."

We brightened. The West Bank!

Fareed said excitedly, "Are we close to Jericho? We are going west."

Hannah warned us, "No, no, the West Bank is in Palestine, and a giant wall surrounds it, bordered by the River Jordan. Follow the river to Jericho and *then* west to Jerusalem.

Fareed asked, "Are there border guards?"

"Yes, but be vigilant, my friends, tell the truth. Possibilities appear when you follow your goals. Whatever your needs, open yourself to receiving it."

Before leaving, Hannah called out, "And don't forget, girls, be one of the boys!"

Follow the River

When we left that day, me in my new (old) trousers and newly shorn hair, I even began to walk like a boy. We tramped in silence under an overcast sky, thankful for the shade. Each was deep in thought. Waves of memory filled the silence; I wanted to forget yet kept remembering.

Suddenly Fareed stopped, sank to his knees, sat cross-legged there in the dirt, and whispered, "Davi always wanted to ride my bike, wanted me to teach him. He kept asking me to read adventure stories to him." His voice intensified. "He had his whole life planned out. He wanted to be an explorer, go around the world, learn how to fly an airplane, and he couldn't accomplish anything!"

He became enraged. "Because of this stupid, cruel, and crappy country!" He pounded the ground with his fists and then covered his face, rocking back and forth.

"You can't—don't blame yourself, Fah-fah," Jadeen uttered with empathy as we dropped to our knees beside him. The three of us, our bodies and arms entwined, gave and took communal comfort from each other.

"We were there too," I said.

"We could have stopped him," Jadeen said.

"But he was my little brother, and all those things I could have done for him, with him."

"And you would have, in time," I said

"You couldn't have known," our sister said.

"None of us knew it would end … that way," I said.

Fareed, his emotions spent, said, "It's time we go." As he stood up, he brushed his hair back and smiled his thanks. We understood.

In a few minutes, he chuckled softly. "Remember the time Davi saw a falling star and we walked for miles over the hills where we were sure it landed?"

Jadeen laughed. "Actually, we all wanted to believe it was a star."

"Then Davi admitted he saw it go *up* before it went down!" I said. "Even then we had to convince him it was a missile."

"Just dumb, gullible kids then, wishing for a star," Fareed said, shaking his head.

We continued to speak of Davi as if he were still alive, just away from them, trailing behind or up ahead exploring the banks of the Jordan River. We were a gang of four again, kindred spirits traveling together once more, toward undiscovered mysteries that lie ahead. As we walked the clouds cleared, and the setting sun gave cause to seek a place of rest.

That night we rolled our blankets close to one another to ease the grief and calm the fear. A clear beautiful evening brought added comfort as we stared at the universe above.

The stars implored the question that I wondered aloud to Fareed and Jadeen. "Do you think Davi is in heaven?"

"Which one?"

"The one with no war."

"Is that the one with seventy-two virgins?"

Fareed said, "Why seventy-two virgins? Isn't one enough?"

"What does God do with them?"

"Maybe that's another heaven."

"Hmm," said Jadeen. "What does a girl martyr get in heaven?"

I said, "They must go to girl heaven with seventy-two boy virgins."

Fareed said, "Davi was a virgin. Do you think he would like a girl martyr?"

Jadeen laughed, "Only if she can ride a motorcycle."

Jadeen and I continued our imponderable babble.

"How many heavens are there?"

"Do we have a choice?"

"I think so."

"Good."

"Why does God have so many heavens?

"Isn't one enough?"

Finally Fareed said, "This is all bullshit."

One by one we fell silent and slept.

Malice of the Deluded

The next morning we washed and drank at the river's edge, tied our bedrolls, and ate bread and fruit given to us by Hannah. We continued southward along the Jordan River on a well-traveled dirt road until we were stopped by two men in a van.

"We're border guards. Let me see your passports," the driver ordered.

"You don't look like guards," Fareed challenged, wary of their lack of military uniforms and nervous conduct.

A bearded passenger suddenly emerged from the van and pointed his gun, ordering us to drop our packs and get into the van. "Except you," he said, pointing at Jadeen, who refused to be left outside.

"I'm going with them."

The man grabbed Jadeen by the arm, pulling her to nearby bushes as she screamed and struggled.

I was terrified. "Hey, stop him. Jadeen is crying."

The driver hollered, "Shut up!"

"I'm going to throw up!" I cried, scrambling out of the van. The man had laid his gun down while grappling with Jadeen's clothes. When I attempted to pick up the gun, it accidentally fired, bringing the driver from the van.

I held the gun in my hands, warning, "I'll shoot you both."

At the same time, Fareed seized another gun from the front seat and joined me. A gun in the hands of an angry girl can be a dangerous thing. I fired at the van, startling everyone, including myself!

"You'd better leave before I fire again."

The men took me seriously. Cursing and scrambling into the van, they sped off!

Fareed and I took turns firing the guns in the direction of the retreating van until empty of bullets.

Jadeen, unhurt, dusted herself off and spat in moral outrage. "Ugly, monstrous men."

"We have to get out of here," Fareed said, still shaken by the narrow escape.

"Yes," I said, "and get rid of these guns." I flung it into the bush.

"Don't you think we should keep them?"

"What for? We don't have bullets."

Still excited and astonished by what had just happened, we ran down the road until we breathlessly collapsed in the dirt. The reality of what had occurred left us whooping and laughing at our fearless acts of heroism.

IV

The West Bank, Palestine

J ust ahead, we braced ourselves for the onslaught of questions sure to come at the checkpoint entrance to the West Bank of Palestine. It looked like a prison, with barbed wire two stories high. Signs of DANGER—ELECTRIC FENCE was posted in three languages.

Three guards watched us as we approached their checkpoint.

"Well, well, where do you think you're going?" they asked in Arabic.

"We're going to Jericho," Fareed answered truthfully.

And then, in a sudden burst of tears, I started telling them our story: leaving Damascus, the refugee camp, the argument at the camp, our Davi, the narrow escape from the two men.

"So that's what all that firing was about? You did that?" one guard asked.

"Yes, they wanted to take us somewhere, and they wanted to hurt Jadeen."

Jadeen reached her boiling point. She tore off her head scarf, her dark hair tumbling around her shoulders, and with controlled fury, she cried, "Hurt me? Hurt me? That man tried to rape me! What's wrong with you men? They had guns, just like you here, the great big man with a gun holding power over kids like us. How can we trust you? Are you not men also?"

"Jadeen, stop!" Fareed yelled.

But there was no way to stop her.

"Do you want to rape us too? You men keep raping virgins here, and there won't be any left in heaven for the martyrs!" She was almost in their faces.

One guard stepped back and started to laugh. The other two guards joined in, and then Fareed and I laughed.

Jadeen turned away, fuming and flushed from her courageous, outrageous rant.

The guard softened. "Those men are scavengers. They want to sell you to slave camps, the girls as sex slaves. Kids like you bring a high price. The boys are trained as rebels or soldiers. Whoever pays the highest price. That goes for girls too."

Fareed said, "Palestine and Israel too."

"No," the guard said, "Palestine and Israel have their own border security. We have our own disputes."

"We have family in Jerusalem," I said. "We just want to pass through. Is that possible?"

We all stood there, determined and defiant.

The guard nodded. "Stay here." He left to confer with the other guards.

He returned with a smile. "You kids are not typical street orphans, and you appear to know how to stay out of trouble," he said with a wink. "Stay by the river, and good luck; you can pass."

He then searched us. As we passed through and thanked him, he called out, "There's a settlement down the river about a day's travel. Look for it." He waved.

———••———

The moon was rising over the river as the setting sun's glow reminded me that we indeed were going south. But no matter, we knew our direction was correct at the moment, and as soon as we reached Jericho we'd go west again. We walked along the road that led to a village by the river. Hungry and tired we proceeded through the streets, pretending we knew where we were going. Then we saw a café of sorts.

"Let's ask them if we can wash their dishes. Maybe

they'll pay us in food," Jadeen said. "We should save our money."

We were feeling rather bold after what had happened that day.

"Okay," Fareed said. "You go first."

Jadeen went inside to test her appeal. Fareed and I waited outside until she returned with bread and fruit.

"How did you do that?" I asked.

"I just said there are three of us traveling south and would be willing to work for food."

"Do we have to wash dishes?" I asked.

"No, just take the food and go," Jadeen answered. "She said no one has ever asked to work for food before, they just come begging. She was so surprised that any kids would be willing to work; most of them try to steal."

Outside the village we found a grassy area beside the river and huddled together for comfort and encouragement. We said our good nights, but before we slept, Jadeen whispered, "I don't know whether to be a girl or a boy. That woman maybe wouldn't have given me food if I were a grubby boy."

Fareed muttered, "I heard that."

Jadeen teased, in a falsetto voice, "Oh, then maybe you should dress like a girl!"

We woke sprawled in the luxury of the warming, morning sun, hungry again. Unleavened bread, no matter how hard and dry, tastes good as long as we had fruit to wash it down. After rolling our belongings, we headed southward.

"Let's get started," Fareed said. "We can't stay here. I hear gunfire."

A wide channel meandering through a barren desert of sand, the noble Jordan River became a guide and savior that restored our bodies and quenched a constant thirst. The abundant life-giving water nourished a shoreline protecting a hedge of green willows and plentiful shade trees, inviting the exiles of unexpected discoveries revealed at every bend.

In this valley of abundance, how odd to witness the stark meager existence of the people we passed. Small groups, families mostly, were camped along the river with clotheslines strung outside tents. Some were shabby huts built from what looked like boards. Kids, just like us, eager and curious, would follow us, sometimes in swarms.

I asked, "Where are your homes?"

"Here, we live here. In tents."

"Why not in the village?"

"The Israelis destroyed our villages."

"Why?"

"Because they want to take our land back."

"Why?"

"Because they say it's theirs."

"What do you do for food?"

"We grow our own, and farmers bring their wagons from the villages downriver."

The conversations were the same. I felt like one of them: no house, refugees on their own land. They looked so hopeful, but their eyes told a different story ... behind the smiles and giggles was a lingering sadness, a hunger to belong.

I was sorry for them yet admired their innocent zeal. At least we had a destination ... well, at least a plan. Yes, the unknown was better than being trapped here in paradise.

The road took a sweep inland, away from the river, leaving the encampments as well. We were alone again without the raucous company of children but relieved of the tension they delivered. That night the sound of gunfire was a constant reminder we were in a war zone.

"Aunt Sonia said stay away from the riverbanks and guns, but how can we when they're all around us?" I asked.

Jadeen added with frustration, "What are they fighting for? What the hell are they fighting for?"

"Their land, each wants to own the land," Fareed said cautiously.

"Why?" I yelled. "Why don't they just all live on the same land without fighting for it? Share the land. The idiots."

"Let's ask someone next time we find a person who has an answer," Fareed teased, avoiding an argument.

Jadeen said, "It can't be that simple. Adults always find a way to complicate matters." Then she added, "Haven't you noticed?"

"Oh, yeah," I said. "I remember when Papa would say, 'Don't squabble; share your pencils and paper,' yet grown-ups fight—only worse, they kill, they don't share, but there's more land than pencils."

Camp WINGS

As we walked the road at sunset, we heard the faint sound of music in the distance.

Jadeen said excitedly, "Do you hear that?"

"It's music; let's hurry." I said breathlessly.

"In a war?" questioned Fareed.

"No one fights to music." Jadeen said. "Let's go."

We ran to the sound. The music led us to the campfires first, then the people, and then to the dancing! The flags! We stood on the perimeter, captivated at the spectacle before us.

A circle of dancers holding hands were stepping in unison to a folk dance. We had seen folk dancers before in Damascus, but only at festivals and never like this!

They greeted us with handshakes and embraces, coaxing us to join in the dance. Musicians strummed and tooted instruments with harmony as we awkwardly tried to follow the dancing. In a matter of minutes we went from cautious to surprise to delight! Without many words spoken, the pulse-pounding rhythm, the clapping, singing, and dancing sent us into another world. Where were we?

It didn't take us long to find out! This must be the village settlement we were advised to look for by the checkpoint guards. For vagrants and strays like ourselves, we became wide-eyed kids again, no longer portrayed as outcasts and misfits. We gladly yielded to this benevolent

Palestinian clan who would liberally welcome and, yes, even embrace people on the simple belief that they honored the rights of all living things.

The three of us were delirious with our good fortune. Many crowded around us with questions asked and answers freely given as best we could. This community was unlike any other we thought existed. We soaked up knowledge like a parched desert quenched from a sudden summer rain.

An open-hearted gentle man stepped forward, a tousled crown of downy white hair and a mustache to match, and affectionately introduced us to his fellow companions. I don't know how Jadeen and Fareed felt, but I loved him. He told us to call him Coach John. He made a sweeping bow, "Welcome to Camp WINGS."

Communication, though haltingly at first, turned to animated body language pantomimed with words we understood, and soon a sort of English-Arabic chatter resulted. Muslims, Jews, and Christians held us spellbound with tales of newsy stories while serving us herbed garlic rice and curried eggs. One girl, named Marla Galana, even introduced us to her smartphone! We instantly became friends. She was a statuesque, slim girl with jet-black hair that framed her delicate, beautiful, amber-tinted face. Within a couple of hours we learned that Marla, her brother, Mathew, and their mother, Sarah, had arranged space within their hostel for us!

Fareed and Mathew, not yet of military age but young enough to arouse a minor distraction to the opposite sex, elected instead to join the men at a nightly communal dinner.

At night, Jadeen and I bunched around Marla with her smartphone. She tapped into Al Jazeera America, a satellite channel that broadcasts news from around the world, including much about the current crisis in Syria. We charged our phones but our calls were blocked.

Marla tried her best to console our concern for our mother and aunt. We were thankful at least that they didn't know about Davi. Later we searched the Internet for The International Humanitarian Aid (IHA) and found a "contact pending, operations under development" message.

I asked Marla about her father. "I never knew my father—he was killed in the US embassy bombing just before I was born in Nairobi. My mother and father met in Kenya when she was serving as a dental hygienist volunteer from the United States. We were raised in Israel and then discovered Camp WINGS. This seemed right for us …"

I lay awake that night, thinking of all that had occurred that day. My last thoughts were of Marla and Davi. Exhilaration and sadness filled my mind as I lay there.

———•◦•———

Daybreak came suddenly. I was woken by the shouts and hoops of the villagers. Fareed was gone, and so was Mathew.

I whispered to Jadeen, "What's happening?"

She was still asleep and barely stirred.

I quickly looked outside to see a few people, including Fareed, pulling down the flags that graced the village. I stood curious in the doorway.

"Go back inside, Tania, we can handle this! A storm is coming, got to get these flags down!" Fareed hollered. He looked so handsome, his dark wavy hair flying every which way.

Waiting for Jadeen to get up, I helped Marla's mother, Sarah, with breakfast. Fareed returned with two flags. One hand-painted in English read

Protect and Teach the Young
Celebrate Life with Love and Compassion
Be Kind and Forgive All

"They certainly practice that," I said. I asked anybody who would listen, "I saw a flag with a rainbow bird—what does that mean?"

Fareed was listening. "You mean this one?" he asked, holding up the rainbow flag. "I recognize many flags in the camp but I never have seen this one."

Sarah, having finished her breakfast, settled back in her chair. All of our eyes were upon her, including Jadeen, now awake.

Sarah began. "That beautiful rainbow bird symbolizes LGBT, some of whom have taken refuge here."

"Who are they?" I asked.

Sarah explained, "Lesbians and gays are those whose primary attractions are toward the same sex. Bisexuals are attracted to both sexes. Transgender is someone whose gender identity differs from their physical birth sex. Transgender people can be straight, gay, lesbian, and bisexual."

"What's straight?" Jadeen teased coyly.

"A person who is attracted to the opposite sex," Sarah replied.

Nervous laughter broke the awkward silence. Mathew had arrived while his mother was talking, and now two boys and three girls exchanged quick glances, hoping no one noticed, but we all did!

Sarah smiled and continued. "All gender preferences are welcome here, just like at the watering holes all over the earth, where species hostile to one another transform that space neutral to all. We welcome those maligned for the color of their skin and cultural beliefs, including people misunderstood for their peculiar genius— artists, musicians, poets, and mavericks, the shunned Romani minority, and the Nomads who journey the land with the seasons."

She paused, letting us absorb her meaning, and then shrugged and smiled. "We're like a circus here, all types of feathers, fur, and footprints, blessed for this sanctuary. WINGS was once an abandoned village nearly destroyed. Now we're in various stages of rebuilding. We have WI-FI, water and repaired power lines, and we grow our own food. Our camp has become an oasis in the storm"

With every new revelation came a spark so brilliant it filled our consciousness with hope that one day that dark hole that burned in our memories might fade and reveal the answers to questions so deep, such as why Davi had to die so tragically.

Mentors and Guides

We found Coach John joined by others that afternoon. Over tea they told us of temples in the east, synagogues of the Jewish faith, Muslim mosque temples in all of Islam, the spread of Christianity, of Catholic priests and the pope, and of the difference between orthodox and sectarianism. Of Tibetan monks, Buddha, and Taoism. Of Eskimos in the north and headhunters in the south, witch doctors, shamans, and burning martyrs at the stake.

More answers brought more questions. Coach John directed these questions to whomever he knew best suited to answer. "Religious wars, the root of centuries-old beliefs, have sadly evolved into hostility and clan warfare in our Mid-Eastern nations ... border wars, yes, and ethnic cleansing ... but now Arab Spring, uprisings in Africa, and Middle Eastern nations. Civil wars are erupting against corrupt rulers backed with military power against oppressed citizens.

"As in your nation, Syria, where rebels rise up against a tyrannical despot who strikes back with poison gas and artillery, sends refugees like your family to the border of another nation. This creates social conflicts. They don't want you; you strain their economy and disrupt their lives. They build barriers, walls, and checkpoints and then fight back with a barrage of bombs and snipers. They must ration food; they blame you for creating hunger, disease, and death. When they are not killing their neighbors, they're pointing guns, shooting at each other in distrust. Ach, what a way to live!"

Another man joined in. "Perhaps you know of an ancient town, north of Damascus, very beautiful, named Maaloula. It is a Christian village where people speak the tongue of the messenger, Jesus. They fight the rebels against your military government. Why? A major highway close by. They destroy a beautiful city for a road? Damascus, Homs, and Aleppo, major Syrian cities, historical and magnificent, uninhabitable now, are being reduced to rubble!"

"What if an army attacks you?" Fareed asked.

John replied, "You can defend, retaliate, or flee—the choice is yours. Free will they call it. Look at it this way. Humans have become so arrogant and swollen-headed that they have forgotten to observe from nature and animals, which by the way have been here much longer than we humans, who are the last to evolve … or digress and stray."

He shrugged and continued. "Animals, when attacked, learn defenses to survive—but some perish. Observe the domineering lion that brazenly kills his offspring. Little does he know that soon his tribe and power will dissolve into extinction except in zoos and animal parks!"

He paused for emphasis. "We who migrate, seeking

a safer place, will prosper. Like you, the three of you. The unknown may not be safer but, I might add, is more evolutionary, wouldn't you say?"

John winked and then continued. "Wild animals live quite well without fences. It's the caged that suffer like prisoners, and some strike back. Sound familiar? We can learn much from our animal friends: the birds that migrate, the fish and mammals of the oceans. Even the butterflies, nature's gift to us, migrate a path just once in their short lifetime!"

"How short?" Jadeen asked.

"Their ballet of beauty, but a few short weeks," John answered. He seemed inspired, encouraged by our questions.

"But let's get back to the human animal. Long ago, the ancients worshiped gods and goddesses—they had gods for everything, even wine! You say enough already! But no, the clans and tribes began thinking of life hereafter … heaven! And a supreme being for their heaven. Conjuring up a mythical god who oversees their chosen heaven alone! Each tribe thought their god the greatest, they argued, they fought, had battles, waged bloody war! Made deadlier weapons, took prisoners, made slaves of them. Oh humans, what foolish humans!"

He paused, sipped his tea, and shook his head. "Any questions?"

I had a question but doubted Coach John would know

the answer. Fareed and Jadeen were intently focused, but my mind wandered.

How did Mathew get his eyes to look like that? As if he could see right through me. And that smile, ever-so-slightly curved on those full, defined lips. And I must learn to cast my eyes downward, like Marla does when she looks at Fareed.

Fareed spoke first, interrupting my daydreaming. "How many heavens are up there, Coach?"

A floodgate opened, verbally battering poor John our mentor. "There are many heavens, if you believe the faithful."

"Who are the faithful?" Fareed asked.

"Those who believe in God."

"Does God live in all the heavens?"

"No, only in the heaven in which one believes."

"How can God be in all the heavens at the same time?"

"Ah-ha, that is the question! That is the mystery! God exists only in the minds of those who think their god is the greatest—and they fight to defend that belief."

"Isn't that dumb?" I declared.

"Yes, but you substitute the word *love* for *god*, and then we eliminate the reason for war between manmade religions."

"That's what my mother said," I replied.

"Your mother is very wise," John said softly.

Fareed asked, "When will the wars end? Who starts these wars? Just when one war ends, another begins."

Coach John lamented with a sigh. "Yes, man's mindless rush to war. I'll answer that with a beautiful question: Does a man need a god for an excuse to wage war?" He waited, but we were silent.

"Who, indeed—men—for power by political corruption, control through religion, wealth for armies and weapons. Most men love to fight, even those who resist, like brainwashed boys and girls who are seduced by false honor. But they still fight, still wage war."

Jadeen snickered. "Fighting is a lot more fun than going to work!"

I had to laugh at my sister's flash of insight, but then I questioned, "What about the women? They don't love to fight."

Coach John said, "What about the women, ah, yes. I ask you, Tania and Jadeen, when will the wars end? When the mothers hold strong. They must teach their young sons that war perpetuates revenge, and then another generation is doomed to kill and be killed. Perhaps that may be the next plateau—*when the mothers, sisters, and daughters tire of bloodshed*—*when they become fierce good haters of war!* Watch closely as the cunning and sly coyote cowers and flees when challenged by the reverence and grace of a deer.

"The great messengers of peace, you know who they are. Through the ages they have been worshipped and revered, they tell us what and why we should be striving for in our life—but they speak in platitudes and dogma. Men must stop preaching and pursue what they do best—build nations, not tear them down. Men are born to *action*, are natural achievers; to invent, explore, compete, farm, produce, protect, and serve as guardians, not invaders.

"We humans are all the same, but men and women are vastly different! Now women are miles ahead of men; they think ahead and can do several things at the same time! They have to, for survival. Women are the real leaders. They give guidance, teach, give comfort and aid, grow wiser all their lives by intuition, not ego. The captain may give the orders, but the women are the true navigators.

"Here's the paradox, one I can't comprehend: men want to protect their own homeland yet invade the homeland of others. That's insanity. They destroy the women, children, and the aged." Our enlightened coach took a deep breath and then exhaled slowly, waiting for a response. We sat spellbound, waiting and wanting more.

He gestured with palms turned upward. "Nature continues to send clues of the natural world in which we live. The reality of our planet, all life, and the beauty of the cosmos will be revealed to us when we are ready. That's the beauty of it all, the mystery of the universe! Go toward the mystery."

Coach John leaned back and laughed. "So for now,

we will have to be satisfied with love, compassion, and forgiveness. Love after compassion and forgiveness."

Jadeen challenged, "Love, compassion, and forgiveness? Aren't these platitudes? Love didn't keep Davi alive."

Coach John, still amused, said, "See, Fareed, I told you women are miles ahead of us." He drew a long breath and then exhaled. "Your love for Davi will always live on. You will find compassion now for others who suffer loss. And forgiveness, yes; you must forgive the hate and evil that surrounds us; this you will learn in time. All of this will come. You are young, so be fearless now. Life's treasures are found when the fearless venture forth … and it's up to you to find it."

"How?" Fareed asked, a bit frustrated. "How can we find a way to end destruction? When will we be ready for the next plateau?"

Coach John leaned forward intently to make a point. "You have already started, my children."

Migrate or Perish

Gunfire heard in the distance was a constant reminder of the conflict on the border. At times the muffled burst of thunder from a missile or bomb blast lit up the horizon.

I was anxious and troubled. *How can these wondrous and worldly exiles live under threats so near?*

I asked Coach John, "Aren't you frightened to live here?"

He answered, "Where would we go? The whole world is cracking up, yes, but we are free—we live on hope and goodwill. Better to die with kindred spirits than to live with those who would have us remain invisible!"

Two days later, after Marla tirelessly tracked down the International Humanitarian Aid Services (IHAS) that had finally located our tent at the refugee camp, we received the message, "The Abu Ali family abandoned their tent, whereabouts unknown." We persisted. Marla called again and again and urged the aid workers to question the neighbors at the camp.

Finally word reached us that the two women said only "they were going west." Fareed was bewildered, but I wasn't.

"Doesn't that sound just like Aunt Sonia? I'll bet they're going to Jerusalem."

———•◆•———

The next morning Jadeen refused food and slept throughout the day. Marla whispered to me, "Look, here's my number, call me when you reach Jerusalem."

"But I'm not leaving here. Not now anyway."

Marla told me I had better speak to her mother. "Something about Jadeen … It's pretty serious," Marla said worriedly.

Marla's mother, Sarah, overheard us. "It's true, Tania, your sister is not well. Maybe an infection."

"What kind?"

"I don't mean to alarm you, but it would be wise to seek a doctor, perhaps a hospital. Maybe all she needs are antibiotics."

"What do you think it is?" I asked again.

With that she hugged me and then whispered in my ear, "I don't know, but you had better hurry to Jericho, where there's a clinic and medical facilities."

Our respite abruptly ended when Palestinian and Israeli gunfire began again, this time close by. This madness of force against resistance was taken in stride by our friends of WINGS. Our beloved settlement hunkered down, but it made us uneasy and I have to admit, frightened. It was time to leave for Jericho, more so because of Jadeen.

Fareed was eager to go. He had been restless and

stood back a bit when Jadeen and I said our tearful good-byes. I worried for Jadeen and I worried for Fareed. Maybe he was feeling responsible for us, a boy with two sisters and a walk ahead of us. Heck, I worried for me too!

But gratefully, the camp members gave us a small boat no larger than a kitchen table.

Coach John said, "Not difficult to maneuver as long as you go in one direction." As he handed Fareed two paddles, he laughed. "The direction of the current."

It was a bittersweet good-bye.

As we pushed off in the tiny boat, our friends on the shore waved and wished us well.

Sarah shouted as she waved the flag of the same message, "Remember, go toward the mystery."

V

The River Jordan to Jericho

The little boat leaked. To worsen matters it rained for a day. Not badly, but enough to keep us wet. What may have been a blissful trip, surrendering to the gentle current southward down the river, we spent wading ashore for cover among the small trees that flourished along its banks.

The rain, in spite of our misery, provided one bit of good fortune. The gunfire ceased. Even the soldiers disliked firing their guns if they couldn't see their target!

We huddled together under a canopy of trees, eagerly sharing food our friends from Camp WINGS had packed for us. As wet and miserable as we were we ate, fueling our bodies with a cornucopia of melons, peppers, tomatoes, and boiled eggs.

Food from friends always makes the body sing.

Jadeen wasn't sharing our enthusiasm. "I'm cold, and I have a pain in my stomach." She moaned, as she hunched over clutching her waistline. She wasn't one to complain, so we had to keep assuring her that Jericho was just a matter of hours away.

Fareed and I cast glances at one another. I told him, when we were out of earshot of Jadeen, the warning Sarah gave me. "Jadeen has to see a doctor. It could be something serious," I whispered.

"We'll get to Jericho soon, don't worry," Fareed said valiantly.

By morning the rain had moved on and for the rest of the day, clouds parted to the gratifying warmth of the sun. By early evening we reached a quay where a few boats were moored.

Fareed scrambled ashore immediately when he saw a couple watching us. Anxious for Jadeen's welfare, he waved and shouted, "How far to Jericho?"

The man shrugged. "A few miles to the west. Just follow the road."

"To the west!" Fareed shouted. "To the west, finally."

He was hardly able to restrain himself as he ran back to Jadeen and me—pointing westward.

Jadeen moaned, "No, oh no, let's stop here." As she attempted to leave the boat, Fareed and I held her until she collapsed on the sandy shore.

The man and woman, curious now, approached us.

"Is she sick?" the woman asked.

"Yes, she needs a doctor," I said.

"Why are you going to Jericho? Are you traveling alone?"

"Yes."

"You are so young to be alone. Do you have relatives?"

"Yes, in Jerusalem. We have a long walk—yes?"

The man enquired, "You will leave your boat?"

Fareed chimed in. "Do you want it? In exchange for a ride to Jericho?"

While Fareed and the couple conversed, I saw that Jadeen was unable to move except for her constant grasping of her stomach.

"Fareed," I shouted, "Jadeen is in pain, and we must do something! She's in terrible pain. She needs a doctor."

Fareed turned from me, pleading with the couple, "Do you know of a doctor, perhaps a hospital?"

The couple exchanged words, and then Fareed and the man shook hands.

Fareed quickly turned, running back to us, and breathlessly announced, "They will take us to Jericho! I've given them our boat."

In our haste, the soggy bedrolls were left behind in the boat. Not forgotten, however, our backpacks, containing our only possessions, stayed firmly strapped, now an extension of our bodies.

Jericho, West Bank

The ride to Jericho was bumpy and thankfully short! Jadeen lay quietly with her head on my lap, her long hair fallen across her pale and listless face. As we approached the clinic, Fareed and I slumped in our seats. It was a very small clinic, a mere house!

Fareed hastened to the entrance and disappeared, returning with a young doctor wearing a white jacket. Thank goodness, that's what we were looking for! He studied Jadeen for a moment and left us, returning with a wheelchair. Once inside, he wheeled her away and then we waited.

What a sight we were! Fareed always looked handsome even after our river experience. Me … well, in pants, a dirty T-shirt, ragged hair, and barefoot, here in the clean and tidy clinic, no wonder we were looked at with pity! I shrugged and stiffened my back proudly. What did they know anyway?

The young doctor came back to report on Jadeen's condition. "Your sister needed several tests, and we have to wait for the results." He quickly looked at Fareed and then me. "By the way, my name is Jacob Kristol. Why don't you two wash up right down the hall? You look hungry. I'll order some hot soup and sandwiches."

We nodded in gratitude. Soap and soup sounded good—we needed both! Then he was gone again. We passed the hour with clean-up and food. Still we waited.

What was keeping them so long? We imagined the worst and then brushed off the "horribles" and decided it was probably just the flu or food poisoning from something she ate.

Finally Dr. Kristol appeared, walking toward us. I then noticed his build: tall and slender with sculptured features. He sat down and leaned forward with an intensity that softened when he spoke, his eyes direct and kind but his face without emotion. "Jadeen's tests suggest a kidney infection, which requires treatment and care at a larger, better-equipped hospital."

"Where? Is it bad?" Fareed asked.

"It could be if not treated soon." Dr. Kristol spoke rapidly, uneasy about the news he was about to deliver. "In Jerusalem, I can drive her there ... but Jadeen refuses to leave without you two, so maybe you can convince her."

Fareed straightened his shoulders. "We can't be separated. We have to go with her—she has no one but us." His demands were more of a plea.

The young doctor sighed, "You three have put me in a dilemma."

"We must go with her, we're family!" I pleaded. "Can't we go in an ambulance, Doctor?"

"If we had one. I'll speak to the resident doctor."

"And you can tell him we have relatives in Jerusalem," I added.

Jacob smiled. "I'm very concerned about her. She's quite delicate." He paused. "And she needs help. How did the three of you happen to be alone, in Palestine at Jericho? And please call me Jacob."

Our eager explanations poured forth like repressed confessions. Jacob offered consoling words uttered with sympathy of losing our brother Davi, and he listened intently as we told him of the refugee flight, the Camp WINGS, Galilee, the border guard incident (which made him laugh), and the Jordan River boat trip that brought us to Jericho.

He shook his head as he stood to leave and announced with determination, "I'll do my damnedest to get you and Jadeen to Jerusalem."

VI

Jerusalem, Israel

Fareed sat in the front seat while Jacob drove his SUV through the West Bank of Palestine. "You kids have been through hell. It's good that you arrived when you did and I was here to help."

"Yeah, I still can't believe it," Fareed said. "But Jadeen—what if—"

Jacob stopped him. "Too soon to tell how serious. She'll be in good hands in Jerusalem. It's not far from here."

"Do you live in Jericho?" Fareed asked.

"No, I live in the Israeli section of Jerusalem. Both my parents are doctors. I grew up with a stethoscope around my neck; no way out of that. I wanted my internship in Palestine, here in Jericho—for personal reasons—Doctors without Borders, that sort of thing. Almost impossible considering the opposition between nations today." He paused and then brightened. "But it's a start!"

From the backseat, listening to Jacob and Fareed, I watched the panorama of barren hills spotted with clusters of encampments, while Jadeen lay quietly beside me. She held my hand, not grasping as earlier, but lightly touching. She was fragile, angelic even. My thoughts grew darker. *We can't lose her too. What if she dies—no, she can't die. Jacob said it might be serious, but what does serious mean? A lot serious, a little serious? She can't die!*

In the distance ahead was a wall as tall as a two-story house. We'd heard about the blockade, either to keep us out or to keep them in.

What did it matter?

What a monster!

It was clear; this wall was meant to divide. I held my breath as we drove up to the checkpoint. Jacob spoke in Hebrew to the guards, and as if by magic, the gate lifted, allowing us through without a search or question. My guess was that doctors must be held in high regard, and it certainly didn't hurt that Jacob was Jewish.

To have come from impoverished emptiness in just a few short hours to this cultured city of prosperous masses was like stepping out of a nightmare awakening to the reality of wonderland. There were soldiers everywhere, only they strolled among the people. Abundance on every corner, cars, buses, women wearing clothes of every description, and the dresses, some long, some short—very short. Like Damascus used to be.

Fareed looked back at us in the car. "I guess we're not in Babylon anymore."

Once again Fareed and I were left in the waiting room, this time in an enormous hospital. Unlike the clinic in Jericho, this one resembled the luxurious lobby of a grand hotel we'd seen in Damascus.

"Can you believe this?" Fareed asked hopefully. "Jadeen is going to be all right."

"In a place like this she'd better be," I said. "What would we have done without Jacob?"

"Who knows? But I do know he really likes her—I mean he *really* likes her! I can tell by the way he looks at her ... and why not? She's our sister, our beautiful sister. He's no fool."

Tired of waiting, I stood up. "Let's go find Jadeen."

The large reception desk was a good place to begin our search for our sister. The receptionist said, "Let me call emergency."

After having been directed to the ground floor, second floor, and third floor, we finally found her. She had tubes leading into her body and machines around her bed.

"Jadeen, we found you; we're here," I whispered.

She looked perky, all cleaned up—even smiling. What a relief! "Jacob just left; he's looking for you." She took a deep breath and then spoke slowly. "It's my kidneys. They almost stopped working. Jacob said the doctors can save them maybe. But I'll have to stay here until I'm well enough to leave. They don't know how long that will be ... I can't go with you."

The news shocked us into silence. The only sound was a gasp and moan from our brother.

"Jacob said I could stay with his parents, who live here in Jerusalem; I want you to continue on to the west, just like we planned. Call Anna Gold at the university. Find Sonia's friends. I'm safe here. Keep going until you're out of danger."

My head was spinning. Leave Jadeen? She was almost giddy reporting her news. Maybe she'd had enough of this sporting life!

It was time for us to leave—to say good-bye.

Then Jadeen motioned for Fareed and me to come closer—our older sister had something to say. Her angelic face smiled again and she spoke softly. "You must remember always ...

"I've been lying here thinking about the mystery— the mystery our teachers told us to seek at Camp WINGS.

Davi's heaven is right here with us. That funny little innocent sprite of a brother ... our love and compassion for him lives right here in our hearts."

She placed her hand over her heart. "We carry his love with us, the love we give to each other. If I never see you again, if I should die, remember my love stays with you. What we learned at Camp WINGS is our responsibility, our fate, to share the wisdom to all we encounter, to forward our love for him to others. That's Davi's gift to us, his legacy."

We stood at her bedside in awe of her composure. Bemused by our concern, she said, "Don't worry about me. I'll be all right." She reached out with both hands and clasped ours.

"We've come far together ... keep going, tell me about the Great Sea—call Jacob and let him know where you are." Then she laughed. "You know where I am!"

Fareed pressed her hand to his chest. "And don't worry about us, just get well ... for us ... and Davi, too."

I squeezed her hand and thought, *I know in my heart she'll be healthy again. I can will her well!* "Jadeen, we'll return soon," I whispered.

———•◦•———

Jacob had been waiting in the doorway, not wanting to intrude as Jadeen said good-bye.

"She'll be fine as long as she continues to receive medical care, and I'll see to that," he assured us. "I've called the university for you."

———•••———

Jacob had taken great care to make sure we had names, addresses, and phone numbers of anyone who could assist us. He reached Sonia's friends after talking to Anna Gold, the dean of student activities at the Hebrew University of Jerusalem. He was ready to drive us to our new destination: Rose and Saul Glaser, Sonia's friends.

Fareed came to my side. "Tania, it's time to go."

Adult Drama, Again

"Sonia and I were students together at the university," Rose Glaser, a plump, pink-cheeked woman befitting her name said as she greeted us at the door. "This is my husband, Saul. Please come in." He was twice as ample as his wife!

Fareed spoke politely. "It's very kind of you to take us in for the night … it's been a very long day."

"Yes, we understand your sister is ill; looks like you'll be traveling without her, a shame. You're going to England from what Dr. Kristol told us," Mr. Glaser said.

"Yes, we'll be leaving in the morning," I said, sticking to the story.

Rose had already set the table for us. "But first you must eat, and then tell us how you managed to travel from Syria to Jerusalem." She shook her head sympathetically. "You poor darlings, such a trip!" She cooed and patted my hand.

My brother slumped in his chair, exhausted, and secretly winked a warning shot at me. "It wasn't too bad—got some rides and a trip down the Jordan River. If Jadeen hadn't been sick we'd be in England by now, where we have relatives."

Mr. Glaser snorted, "You're lucky you made it through the checkpoints in the West Bank. They're turning back refugees pouring out of Syria. Pretty soon they'll be shooting them. Can't trust 'em."

"Can't trust them? Who's them?" I asked.

"Palestinians. Look what's happening. They beat Israelis with clubs, destroy their homes. They want all the land they can steal."

I couldn't help but question his viewpoint. "Whose land is it? Mr. Glaser, it appears to me that wall—"

"That wall, young lady, is there to protect us so *they* don't encroach upon us!"

Fareed cautiously challenged, "Mr. Glaser, we met some very good people in the West Bank, and we heard gunshots all the time from Lebanon, Jordan, and Israel. Seems to me the Palestinian people might be protecting themselves and what little land they have left on the West Bank."

Fareed held his breath.

Glaser pushed his chair back and forced his large body to stand upright, his face swollen with anger.

But before he could speak, Rose slapped the table and then breathlessly exclaimed, "Let me tell you what your aunt did at the university. She was such a rascal, a feminist, she organized campaigns that—"

"Rose, enough, I've heard all about Sonia and your cut-ups! It's late, I'm going to bed," her husband snapped, and he abruptly left the room.

I looked at Mrs. Glaser and thought, *Bless you, Rose Glaser. We are tired and overburdened with adult drama.*

For now, Fareed and I were just two kids sidestepping

the potholes and traps that had snared us. We were a brother and sister driven forward by a will to survive, making choices as we went along the only way we knew how.

Before Rose provided blankets for us in their spare room, she whispered, "Sleep now, tomorrow I'll get you some clothes." She glanced down at my bare feet. "And shoes."

That night in the darkness of the room, we assessed our possibilities and made plans.

"We have to go west to Tel Aviv. It's on the coast of the Mediterranean Sea," Fareed said. "And then find work."

"Okay, smarty, how do we get there?"

"We walk, same as before, or maybe we'll get a ride."

"We don't know anyone there."

"We didn't know anyone when we left the refugee camp. Besides, it's better here—no war here, people are civilized here. Well, some of them. Jadeen is in good hands. Jacob is a good man—he even gave me some money."

"Then we can take the bus!"

"No, we must save it for emergencies."

———————

We bathed and brushed our teeth in the morning. Rose Glaser, true to her word, found clothes for us. I was beginning to enjoy the ratty pants I had worn, but here lots of girls wear jeans, girl's jeans! I felt like a girl again, liberated in my new clothes.

Fareed assured Rose Glaser that we had money to travel to Tel Aviv and then to England. She looked worried, but our confidence convinced her as she took us to the train station and bid us farewell. We hugged her with many thanks for her generosity. She never mentioned her husband.

Crossing Israel Westward

As soon as Rose was out of sight we started walking again, this time in new sandals.

We weren't the only ones trekking the main route to Tel Aviv. We were soon joined by a group of "walkers" who traveled regions of Israel for enjoyment! They *walked* for spiritual enlightenment—what a country!

One of the walkers, a gracious gentleman, said, "We would be honored to have you join us on our pilgrimage—we walk the many paths Jesus took two thousand years ago."

I asked, "Are you walking to the sea?"

"Eventually, but for now we only walk about six miles a day."

I thought that made sense because some members of the group didn't look like they could walk much further, considering their age and ability.

"And where are you headed?" he asked.

"To Tel Aviv."

"Are you walking all the way?"

"Yes, we have relations there," I added.

"Oh, our bus driver lives just outside Tel Aviv and returns at night. Perhaps he can take you there tonight."

And so we walked with them throughout the day—on our own secret pilgrimage. We walked with people from many nations: Europe, the Middle East, Africa,

and America. We walked with Muslims, Jews, and
Christians.

We walked and talked,

Toward the sea,

Toward the mystery.

Our pilgrimage ended that evening at a planned
hostel. The bus driver was there waiting for the tour,
always on call in the event someone needed to cut his
or her walk short, which I thought was very convenient
for the pilgrims.

"Say, could you take these kids to Tel Aviv? They
know where to go," the tour guide asked.

"Going my way, sure enough," the driver said. "Hop
aboard!"

"What good fortune. What great timing!" the tour
guide exclaimed.

We rode as royalty, just Fareed and me in that huge
air-conditioned bus to Tel Aviv.

The driver was filled with good humor, glad to be
going home, I supposed, and clearly loved his job! He was
willing to take us directly to the coast we so desperately
wanted to reach, but he sensed our fear and confusion in
the hectic traffic rush by the harbor.

He offered his opinion. "Look, this is too much city
for you; Jaffa is the historic part of Tel Aviv, not so busy.
I'll drive you there, and if you like what you see, tell me
to stop, deal?"

We trusted him. He wheeled the large bus through the throng of pedestrians and nightclubs, leaving the bustle of the city traffic behind. We entered Jaffa and caught our first glimpse of the Mediterranean Sea!

Sonia's Promise

"Stop here!" we both yelled at once.

"Okay, kids. More like your style, huh?"

We were so excited, we almost forgot to say good-bye after expressing our gratitude!

"Good luck! And take care of yourselves."

Then he was gone, leaving us to stand awestruck at the sweeping grandeur of the Great Sea. An endless expanse of indigo blue as a ribbon of brilliant silver sliced across the horizon, separating the gold-tinted sky. We inhaled its salt air, intoxicating our senses, our spirits soaring even higher.

My brother turned to me. "So this is what Aunt Sonia meant by sending us west to the sea."

I nodded yes. Recalling her words, I giggled. "I remember she said we come from the sea, our Source. Do our tears not taste of salt?"

Approaching twilight, we lingered at the seawall, inhaled the warm, salty air, captivated by the magical ancient seaport village of Jaffa lined with lighted outdoor cafes while boats of all colors and shapes bobbed at their moorings. But we were hungry!

And then, as if by command, a street vendor with brightly painted wheels on his wagon rolled past us, trailing irresistible aromas. In minutes we devoured fresh baked pitas stuffed with roasted vegetables and chicken steamed in garlic and olive oil.

A Harbinger Pelican

When we returned to the seawall, a great white bird was parked in our spot! It was an awkward monster with a large pointed bill held closely at his breast—never had I seen such a creature. We watched him, spoke softly to him. Minutes passed, and then he turned and took flight in an elegant spread of wings, transforming into a mythical giant seen only in our art books. What was that? He flew directly into the night, west!

I was inspired and hopeful for us, even if I didn't know where we would sleep tonight! "He was our omen, a good sign for our future, I'll bet you."

My brother smiled. "That pelican trusted us; he knew we wouldn't hurt him."

"Why do you say that?"

"Birds have instincts; they're more intelligent than humans."

From the seawall we watched nightfall descend as the harbor lights danced and reflected in the water. I became reflective too. This was the first time we had been alone, without adults, without a home. The past was behind us, the future unknown, the present a reward. For that moment, time hesitated.

Fareed and I had been with each other long enough to know (for better or worse) what the other was thinking. Now we had only each other to depend on and care for. I'm grateful for my brother, more so now as days go by.

"Fareed, don't ever die. My heart would break if you died before me."

He laughed. "What, Tania, I'm older than you. I go first."

"By thirteen months!! We're practically twins. We even look alike."

"Okay, I promise I won't die before you, only if you don't die before me—right?"

"Then we will live forever. Promise?"

"Promise."

Almost inaudible I said, "That reminds me of Davi." The subject of death and dying came easy now, embedded in our psyches.

Fareed was pensive and then spoke. "Yes, I think of him all the time. He's with us now, in our memories, his carefree wild way of taking life for granted, as though nothing could harm him. There wasn't a cautious bone in his body. He hadn't learned that there's no such thing as an accident. Lack of caution killed him. His death taught us a valuable lesson—it kept us alive. It's something we—you and I—must never forget, ever."

"Do you want to stay here?" I asked after a while.

"I never want to go back, back to war, to Syria, except to find Mama and Sonia. They're alone in that mess. It makes me angry and sad to think of them. When we do see them or talk to them, we'll tell them what happened to Davi and Jadeen."

I added, "Maybe it's better they not know, at least for a while."

"But for now," Fareed said, "we should keep going, up the coast maybe. To a country that's not in the dark ages! To England, maybe Canada or America. Everyone speaks English now; we're getting pretty good at it. We can work; we know the restaurant business. We can find a place to live, go to school, earn our way."

"Fareed, we need a new story."

"Same story, only now we have relatives in England."

"Where in England?"

"Let's say London."

"Okay."

"And oh, Tania, don't say *God is love* when they ask for our passports."

"I was scared. It was all I could think of—anyway, it worked."

"Well, use it only in an emergency."

"There's always an emergency."

"Don't press your luck, spirit child."

I changed the subject. "Anyway, I'm glad we're leaving. I don't want to stay here either."

"Why?"

"Because of people like Mr. Glaser. Just look at Dr. Jacob. He travels freely between the two states—why can't they *all* do that? It's stupid that two governments can't work together."

"I guess grownups want to keep what they have for fear of losing it."

"But the governments would have more if they shared with each other," I argued. "Like the animals at the watering hole—where all can drink without fear of fighting."

We sat and watched the boats bobbing up and down.

Fareed spread his hands and cast his voice aloud. "Well, we've reached the Great Sea, our destination— here we are. Aunt Sonia, we made it!"

Even the seagulls squawked.

"What's next? What now?" I asked.

The impatient boats beckoned!

Another lapse into silence.

"West, we go west!" I shouted. "Toward the mystery!"

"I was just thinking that myself." Fareed laughed. "To the next plateau!"

I pointed toward the Great Sea horizon. "West is out there!

"Well, let's go out there," my brother announced, and with that he hopped off the wall.

The deck below the seawall on which we sat was an easy invitation. We chose a two-masted wooden sailing schooner with a clean white deck. The accommodations were just right … a cabin, a toilet, and bunk beds! Cradled down below the deck, we fell asleep to the distant music of waterfront cafes.

Part Two

To the West

MAP II – WESTERN TURKEY

BLACK SEA

Istanbul

Izmet

SEA OF
MARMARA

Bursa
▲ Mt. Olympus

Ankara

Canakkale
Troy

TURKEY

Bergama

A
E
G
E
A
N

Izmir

Ephesus
Kusadasi
Didyma

Pamukkale

Termessos
Anatalya

S
E
A

Bodrum

T U R Q U O I S E   C O A S T

Golden Beach

CYPRUS

N

MEDITERRANEAN SEA

50   100   150   200
MILES

VII
Tel Aviv and Jaffa
Israel

"D ad, someone's here."
I was awakened by a boy's voice and then footsteps leading down from the top deck. Shafts of morning sun lit two figures. A man and a boy stood there, looking as surprised as we were!

"We want to go west!" I impulsively blurted out.

"Are you orphans?" the man asked.

Fareed said firmly, "No, we're refugees—from Syria. Our parents are still at the camp along the border. We want to go where the people aren't killing each other."

"We all do! So you are brother and sister, I presume."

"Yes, we have money—we will gladly pay our way to wherever your boat sails." Then Fareed added, "We chose your boat because it's large and seems like it travels further than others around here. It's a beautiful boat!"

The man softened. "My name is Ari Levine. This is my son, Ben. And you are?"

Introductions made, Mr. Levine sat down, and his son, Ben, stood dumbfounded. "Tell me, Fareed and Tania, what if I told you we are going to Turkey, up the coast, to Istanbul, final port. There are rebellions there too."

I said, "Then we will go to England, where we have relatives."

"Why don't you take a train or bus to England?"

Fareed said, "We want to save our money as best we can." (Not admitting we had no passports and wanted to avoid questions from adults.)

"So you want a free ride with me?"

"No, we will work for you, and it is safer by sea than by land."

I added, "And I can do anything Fareed can do, and I take up less room."

"I'm sure you can," Mr. Levine said. "But we have pirates at sea. What makes you think it is safer at sea than on land?"

Fareed squared his shoulders, took a breath, and then answered, "I wouldn't think you would take your son sailing if it wasn't safe, Mr. Levine."

Ari Levine stood up and made a motion to his son.

Oh-oh, I thought, *now Fareed went too far—there goes our sea trip!*

"Call me Captain Ari. Now let's get some breakfast—bet you kids are hungry, huh, Ben?"

Leaving the Levant

That evening, Captain Ari prepared us for the trip.

I asked, "Is this a yacht?"

The captain explained, "Sort of, more like a modified schooner. Called a gulet, it's designed for charter, mainly tourists."

"Will we be sailing all the way?" Fareed asked.

"No, it's safer and faster to motor up the Levant past Israel, Lebanon, and Syria. We're scheduled in a week to meet a touring couple in Istanbul, tour the islands, and then final port back to Israel. Fine weather ahead by reports. I've watched you two today—you're very mature. And I might add you're growing on me. I'm the lucky one. Ben and I could use an extra crew. Tania, are you handy in the galley?"

I answered yes, not knowing what a galley was, but I'd ask Ben later.

"Now, to decide the sleeping arrangements, pick your beds—ladies first. Big day tomorrow."

To say we were excited was an understatement! Instead of one young sailor, his son, Ben, Captain Ari had two more willing mariners he could advise and be assured that we absorbed his instructions. He was a stern captain, but his joy of sailing gave way to bursts of humor that erupted as a sign he was enjoying his role as taskmaster. A slight man, quite dapper, and from a distance, when Ben and Fareed joined Captain Ari, the three of them looked like brothers.

Ben and Fareed became inseparable. I hadn't seen my brother so willing and focused. Captivated by the experience of sailing, he quickly learned the basics: navigational conditions and terms, compass readings, and the importance of climate. He was a natural seaman.

What is it, I pondered, *this irresistible pull of the sea that lures men (and boys) to its unexplored horizon? I feel it myself, that sublime motion forward—unrestricted by streets, lights, and traffic jams.*

I resented the woman's role—condemned to galley duty! The space was tight but efficient, but washing up one meal in time to begin the next wasn't my idea of sailing. I made meals as quickly as I could so I could be topside too. I settled on taboule salad: bulgur wheat in olive oil, lemon juice with cucumbers, tomatoes, parsley, and spices served with pita bread and goat cheese. No one complained.

Anxious to rid myself of galley chores, I climbed topside to watch the sunset. While the constant drone of the diesel engine nudged us forward to Turkey, I'd imagine Mama and Sonia, their faces turned windward, gazing out to sea.

———◦•◦———

As we passed the seemingly tranquil shoreline, we knew land was consumed with bitter conflict and violence.

We dared not stop in Lebanon. A few weeks earlier in Beirut, a car bombing massacre forced us to change direction from Lebanon to the West Bank and south to Palestine.

Tonight, in the blissful refuge of the boat's cabin, the radio hawked the relentless spread of killing. In Tripoli, fifty miles north of Beirut, more car bombings targeted peaceful student demonstrators. Al-Qaeda rebel brigades were holding an entire population ransom by Lebanese sectarian in-fighting. The bordering Syrian civil war had encouraged the Sunni versus Shiite rebels and militant separatists into widening violence and tension, causing innocent civilians to suffer and die.

We stood transfixed in the cabin below as the radio delivered its dreadful news. Thankfully, Mama and Sonia were away from bombings and shootings. Better on the road than in the cities where most of the violence was directed.

The Levant countries bordering the Mediterranean Sea—Israel, Lebanon, and Syria—appeared hospitable, even tempting, to unsuspecting travelers leisurely sailing their coastline. But we knew that something evil had developed on the landscape and was spreading like a deadly virus.

Lure of the Sail

Finally, no longer able to see the distinct skyline of Tripoli, Lebanon's second largest city, Captain Ari called out, "Ben, show our guest crew how to hoist a sail. Going west, my hardies. Heave ho!" Our gulet veered west mercifully away from the coast, its engine now mute.

Suddenly, the wind caught our sail and snatched the hair from my face. The vast sea spread before us, and ocean spray cooled our bodies tempered by the warmth of the sun. Droplets of spray tasted like salt when I licked my lips—or was it my tears? It was a glorious rush, an escape to freedom from the grim events and scenes left far behind us.

We winged our way westward, trailing a line of large graceful white birds that glided past, effortlessly teasing the waves.

"Fareed, look—our friend from Jaffa!"

Captain Ari shouted, "Pelicans, on their migration from Europe back to Africa, they stop in Israel both ways. Magnificent birds!"

Bird migration! I thought, remembering the lessons from Camp WINGS. *Learn from nature; it must be instinct for humans too. Yes, we are migrating just like the pelicans.*

———•◦•———

The contour of Cyprus laid ahead, an awkwardly shaped island with a continuous long finger of landmass sparsely inhabited except for a monastery and a golden beach of sand miles long.

Captain Ari took particular delight in our surprise of the elegant beach, which was ours alone. We spent the night anchored offshore and swam in the warm, clear, silky waters of this ancient paradise where Cleopatra once sailed. Maybe she even swam in this very spot!

On the gulet deck, at night, when Captain Ari and Ben were asleep down below, Fareed and I were left in the vast quiet we hadn't known since we left Syria.

"Do you think Mama will be all right?" I asked.

"Sure, why?"

"Because they're alone without us. I wonder what Mama thinks about Papa and Rashad taking off like that."

"What the hell was that all about? Wanting to go back to Damascus. I think they just wanted to get out of the camp—we didn't even mean anything to them. I don't even miss him, sorry to say!" Fareed dropped his head and then turned, looking out to sea. "When you think about it, we kids really didn't know him at all."

"Did you ever know him? What made him tick?"

"I think he's like all grownups, men really—want to fight, shoot, be the hero. You know, Tania, I didn't want to go back to Damascus. Not because it would be dishonorable to leave Mama but because it didn't make any sense."

VIII

The Turquoise Coast

Everyone woke before sunup, impatient to get the day started. We sailed the turquoise-green sea, the majestic peaks above Mersin, our directional beacon to Turkey. As soon as we were close enough to shore and secured the sail, we slowly motored up the coast.

Captain Ari turned-tour-guide announced, "Turkey, the Cradle of Civilization! Many battles were fought for this land. Cities and cultures rose and fell for centuries as far back to 2500 BC. This country is a natural barrier of sea cliffs, mountain ranges, rivers, waterways, and harbors. One could eat well here. The fertile soil provides grazing feed, good for farming, vineyards, and fruit trees. You name it, Turkey has it!" He then added with a chuckle, "Not much dry desert here, right, kids?"

No, I thought, *not Syria, not the West Bank, not Israel or Lebanon. No, we're not in hell anymore.*

Our world was unfolding with anticipation and intensity as we motored along the rocky cliffs that profile the wonderland of Turkey heading into the western sun.

Antalya, on the Aegean

The seaport of Antalya guarded by lush green hills transfixed the nautical voyagers; a tempting safe harbor and curving bay with many gulets, single- to triple-masted, each one its own personality, proud and stalwart. Closer to port further revealed the idyllic city with palm-shaded boulevards and exotic gardens.

When Captain Ari moored his gulet, in need of supplies and fuel, he announced with gusto, "All ashore. You're on leave, my hardies, but be back by sundown. No staying after dark, you hear? And call your aunt again maybe." He stopped, remembering where they were. "And your sister."

An afternoon off! To our delight, we scurried on land toward the tourist center Mecca, alive with ethnic shops, cafes, and open markets. Surely we'd find an internet café here.

I stayed close to Fareed while Ben chose to wander in and about the crowded bazaar, fascinated with goods and arcade games. We lost him somewhere in the crowd.

Concerned, Fareed asked, "Have you seen, Ben?"

"No, have you?" I said, becoming alarmed.

I thought, *Doesn't he know the rules, always stay together? Where is that kid?* We ran in and out of the booths and stalls, but no Ben.

As I was running with Fareed, a pair of street thugs

approached me; one of them grabbed my arm. "Where are you going, little girl?"

"None of your business! Let me go!"

Fareed, right behind me, was grabbed by the other man. They pulled us into a dark stall and searched our pockets.

"I have nothing, you bastard!" Fareed yelled.

"Help!" I called, but the noise of the street overrode my screams.

"Hey, let us go," Fareed yelled, "we have friends here; they'll find you."

I squirmed away, hitting the man as best as I could. I ran out to the next stall, but no one seemed to notice or care!

I ran up to the man holding Fareed and kicked and pounded him hard. He let go when I punched him in the groin.

They followed us into the street. Fareed spotted a tourist bus, and the driver outside the bus smoking a cigarette didn't notice as we sneaked aboard. The men ran right past us, *the cowards!*

We scrambled to the back of the bus and threw ourselves down, breathing hard, thoroughly shaken. We huddled there when we heard the driver board the bus, followed by tourists returning one by one.

A large man with an open, jovial face proclaimed, "Hey, what have we here, a couple of runaways?"

"No," I said, "some men were trying to rob us, so we had to hide in the bus."

"Are you okay?" he asked, introducing himself as Dexter Wright, an American professor of history. He was seemingly the leader of the tour.

"Yes, we're fine," Fareed replied. "I think."

"Well, lucky for you, lucky for us! Do you live here in Antalya?"

Fareed, watchful and anxious, explained rapidly, "No, we're refugees from Syria, trying to get to England, where people aren't trying to rob or kill us. We came on a boat that's docked in the harbor, but we lost the captain's son, Ben. He's out there somewhere, looking for us."

The exuberant professor said, "Wait a minute. Who's Ben? Oh, the captain's son, you say. Well, at least we know where the captain is—let's go find him!"

Fareed said, "Good, let's find his father and together we'll look for him."

Several members of the tour group had gathered and wanted to join in the search. They followed us down to the dock where the boat was moored. Just then Ben appeared on the boat!

"Hey, you guys, where were you?"

"Where were you?"

This could have gone on and on, no one taking blame. Everyone had a laugh, but Fareed and I didn't share in their amusement. We didn't think it was *that funny*!

Mariners and Professors

The Americans from the charter tour were scheduled to spend the night in Antalya. Quite taken by Captain Ari's humor and good nature, they insisted we join them for dinner that evening.

Dexter Wright, the first to discover us on the bus, cheerfully said, "Good. At seven o'clock, the Rock Cut Restaurant. It's not far from here, just up the street, and bring those fierce sailors, too!"

The four of us washed up. Captain Ari with three juveniles were going to dinner! A sudden panic struck me when I looked at them, all male. They could wear the same pants and shirts and still look presentable for dinner out. Pants are practical. What would I do without pants and pockets? But tonight, for dinner? For a girl? American women dressed in "real" clothes—blouses and slim leggings, some in long skirts, and thick hair, washed and cut from salons.

I was depressed when I looked at myself. I didn't want to go to dinner. But couldn't bring myself to tell Captain Ari, didn't want Fareed and Ben to think I was a silly sissy girl. So I wet my hair and combed it back, tucking it behind my ears. I found a shirt that was Ben's, covered up my T-shirt, and announced I was ready to leave. The three "men" said my shirt looked nice—ha! Nothing about my hair.

We found the Rock Cut Restaurant. It was a large

room, a cave really, cut and carved into a cliff, but it had charm—a charming cave!

Our group sat at one long table, relaxed and attentive, while Captain Ari held court narrating a history of our journey. The three of us joined in with nods and comments, but the captain took center stage while holding the tourists enchanted.

Close by, two women who were particularly intrigued asked for more details, which he gladly offered. They conversed amongst themselves with lots of enthusiasm, Captain Ari laughing and nodding, gesturing with his hands, and on occasion throwing back his head and clapping.

When dinner finished while coffee was served, the two women excused themselves and left our table, choosing a quiet area in a corner. Both women, professors at the University of California, Santa Barbara (UCSB) became good friends, blessed with a joie de vivre and enrichment of travel. Judith Sanford, an attractive blonde, a professor of computer science, and married to a non-traveler, enjoyed the merits touring offered, and Mary Foley was a psychology professor, a handsome divorcee with three grown children. Mary had traveled extensively and boasted it was "in her genes."

As professors, teaching was their chosen profession, but for women, the innate joy of nurturing sprang alive. Fate was here before them; two bright youngsters not traumatized refugee orphans that could be rescued, sponsored, and who could live with us and enter school.

The women returned, came over to our side of the table, pulled out chairs facing Fareed and me, and sat down. Then came the words I had never imagined, not in a million years.

One woman spoke, her face and voice very soft and earnest. "We would like to take you back to America to stay with us." She continued before we had a chance to respond. "Captain Ari told us all about you and your family, that you have relatives in England but you don't know them, only of them. My name is Judith, and this is Mary. We live in California in the United States of America. Would you like to become a part of our international student scholarship program?"

Mary added, "Or possibly an exchange student program with the American Field Service?"

Were they joking? I looked at Fareed, his mouth agape. Words formed but no sound came out. Our past days, weeks flashed in my head.

Tears filled my eyes. The only thing I could say was, "Is it west—of here?"

"Yes," Judith said, laughing. "It is very west of here, far west, on the edge of California on the Pacific Ocean."

Things were happening so quickly. I looked at Captain Ari and Ben, who were grinning.

"What do you say, kids? A chance like this doesn't come along every day. You can't sail the seas forever!"

I agreed. "I'd like to go with you."

I turned to Fareed, and he nodded, "Done." He was sure!

Word spread across and down the table; one by one upon hearing the news they clapped and raised their cups and glasses.

It may be rollicking fun for them, but I had questions. I was anxious and couldn't sleep that night for fear I'd miss something.

———•·•———

We spent our last night on the gulet. Ben, Fareed, and I hovered in a circle on the deck in another poignant parting with promises "of someday soon." Just before dawn we fell asleep there on the deck of our precious schooner.

———•·•———

Below decks in the galley, Captain Ari announced morning by the clatter of pots, his reasonable excuse for a ship's bell. While we stirred, still half-asleep, he appeared before us with a tray of coffee and milk.

"Up all night—can't sleep your day away. Not today!" he declared.

We sipped coffee and slowly indulged in the beauty of the morning, relishing the luxury of comradeship aboard our own private haven, not wanting the moment to end.

As soon as Fareed and I had packed our belongings, refreshed and exhilarated for what lay ahead, I steadied myself to say good-bye—again.

Captain Ari hugged me and then placed his hands squarely on my shoulders and said, "You've been a good sailor, Tania. Now go find your place at the table; the whole world is yours. If for some reason it doesn't work out in Istanbul, call me. I make this trip often; I'll get you back to Israel. Don't forget us—you hear?"

I didn't want to let him go. It seemed we were always saying good-bye to people we loved.

Fareed shouted, "Let's go, Tania! The tour bus leaves at eight."

Waving, I called, "Good-bye, Captain Ari. We'll see you again, I promise!"

"You know where to find me. Good luck in America, Tania and Fareed," he shouted.

IX

Journey through Antiquity

Anticipation of going to America was exhilarating and terrifying. I was unable to sleep or sit still!

I had so many questions, but who to ask? One by one they piled up like stones on my chest until I felt smothered and couldn't breathe.

When Judith and Mary met us at the bus, my first urgent question was to ask them to call Dr. Jacob Kristol, now that we were in neutral territory. The result was the same: blocked call or no signal.

I persisted. "Could you try Anna Gold at the Hebrew University of Jerusalem?" She wasn't in when we called. Well, at least we got through. We left a message as to our whereabouts, hoping she would call Dr. Kristol.

"We'll keep trying," Judith said.

"Ever since we left Tel Aviv with Captain Ari, we tried calling them too, but the message was the same. Blocked call or no signal," I explained.

"Tania, you must understand, Palestine and Israel are considered secured zones. You need special clearance to get through." Judith reassured me, trying to ease my frustration.

On the bus, Fareed and I sat with Judith and Mary, our first opportunity to learn about the charted tour for UCSB faculty, their academic life as educators on campus, and proclaiming once again their *good fortune of our chance meeting and our future together.*

"We don't have passports," Fareed confessed.

"As soon as we get to Istanbul, we'll go to the US embassy and request sponsorship of you both. This is new to us too, so we're all in the same boat. We have confidence it can be done."

Mary offered, "I'll make a call to the embassy to begin preparations," and then she laughed. "If I can get through. We call this red tape. No one likes it, papers, documents, no speeding tickets … just kidding."

———•◦•———

Our first stop on the tour was Termessos, high atop the mountains of Antalya where ruins of agora, the gymnasium and theater, lay visible, shaken by an earthquake in 337 AD.

Then on to Pamukkale, the immense tiers of white limestone that terraced down from warm spring waters, creating a natural spa oasis. Most of the group waded in the water until an untimely wind brought swirling dust—some spa!

They arrived late afternoon in Bodrum, a coastal resort with pristine white condos and hotels that embraced a harbor amassed with alluring low-board schooner gulets for hire, tempting the tourists. Dexter the history professor couldn't resist; chartering a cruise for the evening with ten others from the tour, they leisurely motored past nearby islands of the emerald-green Aegean Sea.

Dexter, remembering his love of sailing as a boy, was quite impressed by Fareed's knowledge of the gulet.

"For a young man who's lived all his life in Syria, you sound like an old salt!"

Fareed was flattered. "I like it! It's amazing how much you can learn when you really want to and are inspired by it. I would be happy owning a gulet, just like this one."

"I would too—what a life!"

And with that Dexter and Fareed became friends, exchanging views of history and the merits of seafaring.

Fareed asked, "Where in California is Santa Barbara?"

"It's on the coast, a beautiful city."

"Does it have a harbor, and boats?"

"Yes, all kinds—yachts, sailboats, and power boats."

"Gulets, like this one?"

"Not exactly, but similar! I'm partnered with a friend who has a large sailboat—he's also a friend of Mary's, your sister's sponsor."

"Maybe we can go sailing together?"

"I'm sure we will, mate!"

"I wonder what America is like," he thought aloud.

Heading back to Bodrum, Dexter and his wife, Karen, discussed sleeping arrangements for Fareed.

"Fareed, good news, my man. Karen and I would very much like to have you room with us."

Karen joked, "If you don't mind a sofa bed."

Fareed found kindred spirits with the Wrights.

———•◦•———

After Bodrum, the tour traveled to the Temple of Apollo in Didyma, colossal skeletal remains of a great temple started in 300 AD. It was an entire city of 120 massive carved marble columns and stone stairs, some still in place.

We bused to the international resort town, Kusadasi, with beautiful sandy beaches, close to the Temple of Athena, the most preserved classical city in Turkey, and then on to Ephesus. Dating back at least 3000 BC, it is only one tenth restored, an excavation ongoing.

We had become unexpected surplus-turned-celebrity guests for the tour members who would hurry to our side, seeking accounts of our journey west from Syria. What did we know of the Assad regime?

What were the refugee camp conditions?

What about our family and restaurant in Damascus?

Were we frightened venturing out into the unknown?

Then with earnest, sympathetic eyes, they expressed profound regret when we recalled the loss of our brother Davi and concern for our sister in Jerusalem.

When we told them of our mentors at Camp WINGS, a communal outpost in the West Bank, enthralled as they were, a skeptical few doubted there was such a place! We in turn were equally curious about America.

How large is the United States?

Does the United States go to war?

Why does the United States have so many presidents?

What is democracy?

Do Americans all believe in the same thing? Like one religion?

Is everybody rich?

Do Americans have bombings and killings?

Why do all Americans have guns?

Do they kill each other?

When we stopped for lunch or sightseeing, the tour members as well as my brother and me never missed a chance to try to call Dr. Kristol or Anna Gold. Most of the time obtaining a signal in a moving bus was difficult enough, but when we reached a party, we could only leave a message—there was time though.

Our gregarious Dexter, a natural teacher, had become fond of Fareed, like a son he never had. Fareed stayed close by, now considering him a brother, maybe an uncle with whom he could confide.

Karen, his wife, was delighted to mingle with the women, not all that able to climb the stone stairs of ancient ruins and gape with wonder at yet another marble column.

On one such walk, Fareed felt free to express his frustration when Dexter asked, "Well, ancient mariner, what do you think so far of us Americans? Ready for America?"

Fareed answered, "These Americans are fascinated with ancient ruins—we live in a museum! We live among ruins, all over our country; it's not new to us. I'm not thrilled by them. The Babylonian Empire was all over the mid-east—1900 to 700 BC. The capital city, Babylon, in Iraq—look at it now, in ruins again. Aren't you weary of it? I am! Doesn't that tell us something? History keeps repeating itself. America is just a few hundred years old. It's a young country. It could happen to them. I want to go there before it blows up!"

Dexter chose his words carefully. "It's a new world now, not better perhaps, but different. America is a democracy, a land of many faiths and beliefs. In America they have a Constitution that separates church and state. And a Bill of Rights. Equality and human rights for all. In America, people are free to believe in what they wish. It's messy, but it works.

"Now, the Islamic faith is their moral mortar. Islamic law is based on religion, culture, and politics that binds strict and devout believers—separates all others who don't follow the rule of the Koran. Those who don't follow? Then we have violence and death, jihad, holy wars."

There would be much to learn from each other.

——————

The tour bus navigated through the large city of Izmir for a lunch stop at an outdoor café on the seafront promenade. Mary, Judith, and I chatted together at our table while we held their cell phones intently calling our numbers, now memorized.

Mary sought a private, quiet area indoors and called the US Istanbul embassy. When she returned, her face marked by self-restraint, she said, "I just spoke to a woman at the embassy. She's sending me an application for appointment. She said in order to get a student visa scholarship program from here, both spouses must sign for Fareed and Tania."

Judith gasped. "Well Mary, you're single, no problem there, but Gunnar hates to fly and it would take days to get here! What do we do now?"

"I have an idea," Mary said cryptically as she stood up quickly and left. Sitting at a table nearby, Mary joined Dexter, Karen, and Fareed and explained the problem.

Dexter burst forth with a flourish. "Hell, there are a dozen people on this tour who would qualify, who would trip over themselves to sponsor Fareed, but I'm first in line! Huh, Karen?"

Karen clapped her hands. "It's kismet!"

Fareed was chagrined, and he released a genuine chuckle.

That evening at dinner, all who were present toasted Fareed and me and celebrated the new arrangement with much attention and fanfare. Dexter and Karen were especially exuberant!

After the toast and dinner, I excused myself, leaving for my room. I grew melancholy and then moody and nervous. I worried about Mama, Sonia, and Jadeen as we hadn't reached them yet. News of the growing crisis in Syria was headline news. I tried calling the numbers.

Fareed came in. "Tania, why'd you leave? Are you sick?"

"No, I'm worried, that's all. You know."

"Look, we'll be in Istanbul tomorrow, at the embassy. We'll receive info from the IHA then, so don't worry, okay?"

"I'm really happy for you, Fareed. I love Karen and Dexter, and Mary is so worldly and generous. Fareed, I wouldn't have left if you didn't have a home too. I would have stayed right here with you! America or not!"

"Well, that's not going to happen."

"You know, in spite of all the luxury around us, I'm scared—what will happen next? Maybe we can't go. Just when I feel safe, something happens, something unpredictable and shocking. Are we ever going to be safe again? Maybe we shouldn't go to America, a strange country; maybe we should have stayed in Israel. I don't want to go to America. It's too uncertain, something might happen ..."

"Tania, that's the point. Something *will* happen, and we'll deal with it when it does. Hey, don't you think I've been thinking that too? But look, I feel like I'm on another planet. We've been through hell and back. You know that. When we were on the gulet with Captain Ari, I felt like we had reached some peace, sailing away from all that ... that ..." He hesitated and then shook his head.

"When I look and talk to these Americans, they don't know anything about what's going on here; they don't even care. They laugh, eat, and buy things like nothing bothers them. Turkey is just across the border from Syria, our country, a war zone. Is Turkey next? Uprisings are spreading; every day innocent civilians are caught in clan warfare … we have leaders who care nothing for their people! Innocent citizens, their soldiers and politicians that murder their own neighbors—and for what?"

He stared at me as if I had the answer, and then in disgust he added, "Arab Spring—ha! It's been going on for centuries. Step on one anthill and another forms!"

"You know what I think, Fareed? Our Middle Eastern states need to get our act together—don't we know these battles can't keep on forever? Is it just a way of life? We just love to fight! What is it that we are doing wrong? What is America doing right? That people can travel to these countries, tour, visit, and then leave for home to all their luxuries."

My brother spoke earnestly. "That's why I want to go to America, to find out what makes it work. If we go, Tania, I want to find out and then return in a year maybe, find Mama, Sonia, and Jadeen—maybe someday we can make a difference. Go to school … make it better for our country."

My spirits rising, I agreed. "We've been lucky. Maybe we were born for a reason, maybe destiny—to right the wrongs that are happening now."

"We can't be the only ones," he said. "There are lots of kids like us who have experienced what we have—surely they want to change it too. I'll find them when we return." We all grew up before we were grown up.

"It's up to us, Fareed, the younger ones, our generation, who have lived through it."

Fareed, smiling now, said, "As Coach John said, 'When the people have had enough.'"

"Go forward to the next plateau."

"To the mystery," he said.

"Deal?"

"Deal!"

Elated, we hurried downstairs to join the celebration.

"Hey, where have you been? This is your party, kids."

"Talking politics!" Fareed said.

"Solve anything?" Dexter laughed.

"It's a glorious mystery," I said.

Members of the UCSB bus tour boarded early the next morning for the two-hour drive to Bergama, an ancient Hellenistic city near the Aegean coast.

Fellow passengers, albeit immersed in the Asia Minor historical period, had become distracted by recent events occurring in present-day Turkey. In Istanbul, demonstrations had erupted from long-smoldering political corruption that produced a mixture of excitement and anxiety within the tour group. They were impatient to return home.

Every bit as eager, my brother and I were about to venture on our own odyssey of discovery to America that did in fact conjure up a poignant real-life journey amongst our scholarly, learned friends.

The cadre of six had become the center of attraction; seated now in pairs on the bus, Dexter and Fareed, their heads close together, spoke about the wonders of sailing. Karen and Judith chatted about the rejuvenating powers of Turkish baths.

With a two-hour drive ahead, Mary, seated next to me, had allowed some intimate time with my soon-to-be house host. I couldn't resist this opportunity to question my curiosity about American women; this seemed the perfect moment to ask, "Who are the women in America that girls admire most?"

"You mean celebrities?"

"No, I mean women who speak out against injustice and aggression, who have courage, are bold, you know, who lead"—and remembering Coach John's words— "and who are *good haters of war*?"

Mary explained, "Some celebrities use their fame for a cause they believe in, that takes courage and they're ridiculed too. But that doesn't stop them; they just keep going."

The professor of psychology seemed impressed by my assertion.

"But whoa, that's some question—well, there are many. I could name a few of my favorites, but let's do this, let's ask the folks on the bus to name some, okay?"

"That sounds fair."

"Okay, you ask them."

I stood up in the aisle of the bus and in my best English asked for a response. At first they smiled, and then they laughed. But they could see I was serious, so the names began. Eleanor Roosevelt, Sally Ride, Maya Angelou, Oprah Winfrey, Hillary Clinton, Gloria Steinem, Rachel Maddow, Melinda Gates, Ann Richards, Jane Fonda, Barbara Walters, Michelle Obama—many I had never heard of.

Fonda brought a few whoops, but Mary countered, "She earned her stripes and she was right as it turned out. Lyndon Johnson was skeptical about the Vietnam War; she had the courage to act on it."

I was exhilarated. This started a discussion that lasted until we reached Bergama, another site of antiquity. Upright marble columns, some still standing, some fallen and resting since 3000 BC lay scattered about—brought a few yawns!

I Will Remember Troy

After lunch, refreshed and relaxed, not many were enthusiastic to board the tour bus again. Travel weariness prompted a vote by the group to bypass Troy and hurry on to Istanbul.

The Turkmen tour guide was clearly annoyed and said, "You came all the way from America to Turkey and not want to visit *Troy*?"

He shamed them! So we went to Troy, where excavations uncovered nine cities layered beneath today's Troy, the remains of which are at eye level. The first settlements were around 3000 BC. Troy IX vanished around 500 AD. The only thing above eye level and standing is a huge replica of the famous Trojan horse. So many battled here for this historic city, now nobody wanted it, except archaeologists.

While counting the layers of Troy that resembled Greek spinach pie, *spanakopita*, and right there in the excavated open dig of ancient Troy, Judith's phone played its ring tone alert.

It was Jacob! The long-awaited connection!

Judith called out, "Got Jadeen! Tania take the phone, I'll get Fareed."

I ran to Judith's side.

"Jadeen, is that you? How are you?"

"I'm all right. Where are you?"

"In Turkey, at Troy. We're okay."

Eager to relay the news, Jadeen spoke quickly. "Aunt Sonia and Mama are in Northern Israel ... they're traveling to Camp WINGS, following our route. Sonia received word from Uncle Rashad. They joined the rebel fighters, have come under attack from terrorist armies but can't disclose their location."

"Jadeen, does Mama know—"

"Tania, they know about Davi," she whispered.

A long silence hung heavy between us. Neither dared speak.

Jadeen finally said, "They backtracked to Safed and found the village and the rabbi who took care of us. He told them what happened—walked them to the grave. There were flowers already planted by his headstone."

"Flowers, flowers ..." I murmured. "I will plant a tree ... a tall tree when I return."

Jadeen continued. "I told them you were safe. Is that true? How did you get to Turkey?"

The connection was breaking up.

I answered, "It's a long story," and then added, "Do you have Marla's number from Camp WINGS? We must talk to Mama and Sonia before we leave for America. I'll tell you more later."

"Yes," Jadeen said. "I have her number; I'll call Marla to watch for them."

By now Fareed was by my side, giving me hand signals.

"Call me if you hear, okay? Fareed wants to talk to you."

"Hey, Jadeen, are you still living with Jacob's parents?"

"Yes, they are watching me closely, I read all day long. I'm an expert on kidney disease now." She laughed. "I've become ... medicine ... student and study ... a doctor."

Fareed said, "Next plateau, sis." The phone went silent.

I'll always remember Troy with mixed emotions!

Perhaps it was the early morning hour of the last day, not travel fatigue that restrained and subdued the troupe to utter salutations in hushed voices. Except for Fareed and me, whose expectations of the unknown brought forth heightened excitement, and soon the entire busload became animated and boisterous, enveloped by the fever of youth.

While at the same time, midday at Burza, an architectural, artistic city rising from the Roman and Byzantine periods, resting at the foot of Mount Olympus brought further anticipation; a lunch stop always guaranteed a flutter of activity that ensured food and the welcome bathroom sign. We were on our way to Istanbul.

X

Istanbul, Turkey

As Fareed and I beheld the magnificence of Istanbul, our anxiety grew, despite the imposing splendor of the mosques and towering minarets, and the Galata Bridge crossing the Bosporus peninsula of Asia Minor. The energy that pulsated throughout the famous gateway city only heightened our stress as autos, buses, and pedestrians tangled with pesky street urchins determined to barter goods easily obtained at the Great Bazaar!

The tour group continued on to scheduled destinations of historic sites, leaving the small cluster of hopefuls at the gates of the US embassy.

The American professors were confident that documentation was a formality they could deal with successfully. Fareed and I weren't so sure, given what we had been through; our angst was palpable. We grew silent and withdrawn, intimidated. Another barrier, another checkpoint, another giant wall, obstacles that could destroy our hopes and expectations.

Our fears were realized; security protection systems began with the embassy guards at the gate. Our first barrier. With guns drawn, they ushered us into a secured house and then photographed and scanned everyone by X-ray. In addition, they searched and inspected all our electronic devices and documents. By phone they relayed to the US consulate general for proof of appointment.

An hour passed. Dexter assured us this was a matter of protocol, that embassies were targets of terrorism spreading now into Turkey. The long wait was over when we were cleared to pass through to the main entrance, a fortress-like building guarded with secured vaulted doors.

The US consulate general greeted us at his office door, this gesture a surprise given his importance—a man who could grant or refuse our needs with a stroke of his pen.

Mary and Dexter made the introductions and then proceeded to define our desires. Dexter was magnificent in detail, this warmhearted, jovial man turned into a force of masterful explanations, adding pathos when needed, anger when justified. He pled for "sanctity of life" and proposed that "Syrian students living in

America will be the voice of millions of refugees created by tyrannical aggression and bloodshed."

The force of his personality and earnest convictions were enough to sway the most unyielding of juries. As I listened, spellbound by the professor's eloquent and persuasive quality of reason, I thought, *He convinced me!* I had just observed the spoken language of men; by virtue of mutual respect are able to negotiate, compromise, and agree. They were the picture of diplomacy.

The consulate general listened, nodded, and smiled, his stern face determined behind his eyeglasses. He sat frozen, and then, taking a moment to remove his glasses, replied, "I admire your request—what you're asking for will take six to eight weeks to accomplish. Are you prepared for that?"

"Absolutely not!" Dexter responded.

The consulate general laughed. "I thought not, but perhaps instead of a student visa for these two minor refugees we can issue an emergency permit based on humanitarian asylum ... provided you are willing to be bond holders responsible for minors."

They all began to exhale—the professors nodded in agreement.

The consulate general added, "You can apply for student visas when in America. You have six months for application and your passports, now—you will have to remain here for a couple of days while the papers are finalized."

"We will enjoy your city," Dexter said, "and your hospitality with pleasure while we wait."

Then as more information was required, questions and answers and signatures all around, Fareed remained stoic, whereas I, on the other hand, was just barely able to hold my composure.

———————

Our tour group was elated by our news when we met that evening at our hotel, but disappointed we couldn't join them on our flight back to the states. Judith decided to fly back with the tour, promising to see Fareed and me at their respective homes in Santa Barbara.

In the lobby early the next morning, the tour group assembled, dressed in comfort for the long flight home. Good-byes were unusually cheery and upbeat, even for those who didn't relish flying. This time parting farewell was an ecstatic event for Fareed and me. We would see them again, our family of friends flying to the other side of the world! As the group boarded the airport shuttle, they called out, "California, here you come," "On to your next plateau," and "See you on campus!"

We were quite alone now with two days to explore the brilliance of Istanbul. Exhilarated by the task of successfully granted passage of their wards, we decided to dine, relax, and begin a day of touring in the morning.

We walked the bustling streets of Istanbul and inhaled the exotic spice scents at the covered Great Bazaar, where we strolled past hundreds of vendor stalls of jewelry, brass, and Turkish wares. Hailing a cab, we marveled at the colossal Blue Mosque with six minarets!

"No excuse for not hearing the summons to prayer," Dexter pointed out.

We then proceeded to the Church of Hagia Sophia in all its grandeur, equaled only to the palace of Topkapi, although challenged in size by the enormous mosque of Sultan Suleyman. From the balcony of our hotel, we viewed the Galata Bridge, when, as night fell, paraded a constant stream of traffic glitter, autos, cruise ships, and ferry boats gathered at the harbor hub—a steady motion of glinting and reflecting lights.

That night in our room, Mary received a text message: *Jacob and I driving to WINGS. Mama and Sonia just reached camp. Staying with Sarah. Tired but thankful. Will arrange Skype conference when we arrive. Love, Jadeen.*

When Mary showed the message to me, after much jubilation, she asked what I would want to reply. My mind was spinning. *They made it! They're safe—with Sarah! Oh, what to do?* "I'll be right back! Got to tell Fareed!"

"Tania, wait, let's text Jadeen now! Tell Fareed afterward."

"Okay, tell her we're leaving for America day after

tomorrow. To call or text as soon as they arrive at WINGS! Oh, and tell her we love her and Jacob and Sarah and—"

"I know, I know." Mary laughed, "Now go tell Fareed the news while I send your message!"

I ran down the hall calling, "Fareed! Dexter! Karen! I have great news!"

———•·•———

Dexter and Fareed left early from the hotel to visit Old Istanbul, the central portion of the newer city. Mary, Karen, and I stayed close to the hotel, not wanting to miss any calls from the embassy or Jadeen. As much as I tried to relax, the tension and excitement grew as we prepared to depart in the morning. When Dexter and Fareed returned from their tour of Old Istanbul, flush with history but current news of organized demonstrations against political corruption in Ankara, the capital of Turkey, worried him.

Dexter announced firmly, "We're getting out of Turkey just in time. We don't want this—there's enough going on of this nonsense, even back home. Let's go to the embassy and give them a push."

"Good idea," Fareed said. "Let's go. But could we just eat first? There may be a long wait again."

He was right. The inspections and permits took the

better part of the afternoon—time was now passing quickly. It was nearing early evening before they were able to secure our documents. And when presented to Fareed and me, it was performed somewhat as a religious ritual. The clerk who administered the oath granted their promise to obey the laws of this coveted permit; a solemn ceremony by which we were willing to swear and obey, albeit equally gratified the ordeal was over!

That evening in our room, I stared at the phone on the table between our beds. Still no word from Jadeen. "Mary, how does Skype work? Will we really be able to see them and talk?"

"Yes, if we can make connections. I'll text Jadeen, set up a Facetime."

"I won't sleep tonight. I can feel it."

"Yes, you will—well, eventually. I don't think they'll call if it's too late, so rest now, chickadee, big day today, huge day tomorrow," Mary assured me as she turned off the light.

The room, now secure and warm, glowed from the city lights of Istanbul below.

Mary spoke softly, almost a whisper, "Tell me about your mother and Sonia, about your family."

It was the first time someone wanted to know what I thought, how I felt—without bias or judgment. A flood of memories awakened stories two friends could share, intimate secrets only women would understand. We were getting to know each other. The bonding essence of compassion and trust was beginning. In my short life, after months of restless nights, I sank deeply into sleep—a smile on my lips.

The Last Day in Istanbul

Morning came quickly. Fareed, Karen, and Dexter were already downstairs when Mary and I joined them.

"All packed, everyone?" Dexter hailed. "Let's get to the airport early; you know how check-ins are. I don't want any trouble from security questioning our documents."

"We're ready," Mary said. "Oh, Dexter, I'm going to set up Facetime with Jadeen about eleven this morning. Time about right?"

"Should be wild! Hope you can connect!"

Fareed joked with the young driver as he helped load our baggage into the rear of the cab. As we drove through the streets of Istanbul on our way to the airport, I was reminded of the sidewalks of Damascus. Inclined to daydreaming, I gazed at Fareed's profile and pondered how much I loved him, Jadeen, and Davi. How innocent we were then—those delicious, untroubled days and nights as we scouted the city shops and sights of Damascus. Four kids, linked at birth, and united as a team, unbreakable. We challenged, trusted one another, and grew increasingly emboldened and confident ... and fortunate! Could any of us have done it alone? I thought not.

As I reflected on those free-spirited days in Damascus, I grew melancholy knowing those years would never come again. I would never be a child again.

Suddenly the cab lurched to a stop in traffic that startled me. Recent events sped through my mind, an odyssey of heartbreaking images, all too familiar now, tragic pain-filled assaults by forces of evil intentions and intimidation, obstructions and barricades forbidding our passage. Yet clearly, somehow charity and tolerance from others prevailed, raising hope and determination to keep moving forward. I fantasized, "Can a girl and boy stop or prevent a war? No, but perhaps a team, an honorable team!" Just as Dexter had said to the consulate general, "Two Syrian refugees could be the voice of millions."

———•◦•———

We arrived early at the Istanbul International Airport. Dexter, Karen, and Mary knew their way around, comfortable as experienced world travelers; however, Fareed and I were aghast at the confusion and hustle of the crowd.

Mary call out, "Stay close to us, losing you two now ..." Her voice was drummed out by the clamor of activity.

We checked in, passed through security without much trouble, except for glances of puzzlement, and then well wishes from the guards. Someone mentioned food, remembering we hadn't eaten yet.

As we rode the tram to an indoor café, the parked

planes visible from the windows, Fareed didn't hold back his wonder. "I've never seen a jetliner up close; how can anything that huge get off the runway?"

Dexter said, "Just wait, it's amazing."

Just as we settled in at a restaurant table, Mary's phone rang—maybe, just maybe it was Jadeen!

"Look." Mary held out her phone. "Do you know these women?" It was a Facetime video on her phone of Jadeen, Mama, and Sonia, arms about each other.

"They're with Jadeen!" Fareed shouted. "They made it! And look, there's Marla and Sarah."

Then Jacob appeared in the background with Mathew.

"We're here at WINGS. Jacob brought his laptop so we can talk to all of you," Jadeen said excitedly. "Here's Mama."

A familiar voice and face became visible up close. "Mama, is that really you?" I cried.

"You are going away? To America?" she asked.

"Only for a little while; we'll be back soon, Mama, maybe in a year. But Mama, you and Sonia followed our path. How did you do that?" Fareed asked.

"Oh, Fareed." Mama laughed. "I couldn't have done it without Sonia; such a wise sister."

"Will you stay at WINGS?" I asked.

"If they'll let us," Sonia joked. "And then we'll move on to Jerusalem," she said as she popped her head into the image. "I have my associates and friends at the university and Jacob and Jadeen. Now tell me, who are these people, these professors. Are they trustworthy?"

Fareed laughed. "Here, Aunt Sonia, you judge for yourself. This is Professor Wright and his wife, Karen, and Professor Foley."

They took turns introducing each other, very excited to share some anecdote about Fareed and me.

Our group turned quiet.

Jadeen reappeared on screen. "We told her about Davi, what happened and how."

"It's true," Mama uttered. "I've had my tears."

Composed, I said, "We couldn't stop him. Please forgive us … Davi is with us, he never left us. We will always have Davi with us—"

"This war, killing, bombing, our children, I don't understand." Mama vanished from the screen, wrapped in Sarah's arms as Marla said good-bye. "Call soon or write, whichever is quicker. We love you," and then she was gone.

Jacob and Jadeen came into view together. "We will stay in touch, write every day, go forward."

Then Sonia's face reemerged. "We met Coach John—a wise and spiritual man—and very fond of you three. He sends this message: 'Travel well to your next plateau.'"

Fareed responded, "We will, and thank him for us."

He swallowed hard; it was difficult for him to speak. "We'll be flying west, just as you told us." Then came that familiar chuckle, he added, "But it was you, Aunt Sonia, who led the way."

Epilogue
Early Summer 2015

Somewhere over the Aegean Sea, an airliner flew southward to Israel. Inside the extensive cabin, Tania, with dark short hair, bobbed and tucked smartly behind her ears, gazed out the window. Far below she glimpsed Istanbul, from where they left many months ago. Her eyes focused on a line of white specks that glided gracefully over the turquoise-blue Aegean Sea. The great white pelicans were on their migratory passage once more. Tania smiled, remembering.

She reached across the aisle. Her brother's hand met hers. They clasped tightly until a flight attendant appeared, causing their hands to part. Fareed adjusted his position to accommodate his long legs. He was restless and found it difficult to remain comfortable. A newspaper dropped from his lap, exposing the bold, black headlines: **Global Terror Expands** … *until the people tire of war*, he thought grimly.

The airliner slowly descended toward Tel Aviv, where their family waited at Ben-Gurion International Airport.

Tania and Fareed were anxiously eager to share their news of wonder and discovery in California; three semesters at Dunn School with the International Students Program and plans for college at UCSB.

Throughout their absence, communication with their kindred relatives was nonstop by long letters, e-mails, and joyous, tearful telephone calls. Now the longing vanished, replaced with suspense and impatience to behold their family once again.

Dr. Jacob Kristol found a charming, balconied apartment for Rama, Sonia, and Jadeen. Under Jacob's watchful eye and devoted care, Jadeen continued to flourish. She attended school to further her medical studies in Jerusalem of which she exclaimed, "No other city so divided thrives as this—because we must."

Rama, animated and beautiful, now transformed in modern dress, relished her newfound life in Jerusalem. Sonia accepted her previously held position at Hebrew University. She now emboldens her students to always strive to seek their next plateau.

Captain Ari and Ben hosted several tours for the family, including Jacob who had discovered the lure of the sail.

Khaled and Rashad are somewhere along the northern border of Syria. Sonia has received messages but was unable to respond.

Humanitarian Agencies

UN Refugee Agency
www.unhcr.org

UNICEF—United Nations International Children's Emergency Fund
www.unicef.org

UNHCR—United Nations High Commission for Refugees
1-855-808-6427

IHA—International Humanitarian Aid
www.internationalhumanitarianaid.org/

WFP—World Food Programme
wfpusa.org

IRC—International Red Cross
www.icrc.org
1-877-843-7090
International telephone +4122-734-60-01

IRD—International Relief Development
ird@ird.org
1-703-248-0161

Acknowledgments

First and always, my heartfelt gratitude to my husband, Don, for his patience and accepting my necessity for solitude while writing, yet he was always at my side willing to offer, "Dinner out tonight?"

It would be futile to put into words thanking the friends and colleagues who inspired and encouraged me in the course of writing this book. But there are a few who were consistently there.

To begin, I must acknowledge the devotion and support I received from my families, which are paramount. My boundless thanks to the Courcier family: Rich, my daughter Jennifer, and their two girls. Both in their twenties, Lexie provided valuable insight, reminding me of what it was like to be a thirteen-year-old girl again. Sydney, a recent grad student, did an amazing job expertly editing my manuscript.

With deepest love and profound gratitude to my son Ryan and his wife, Jill, for our lively conversations and revelations into our blended-family dynamics and history that moved the story along.

I am deeply moved by the uplifting enthusiasm from Whitney Bell, my granddaughter and CC literary mentor/writer. Her calls have elated me with her work and feedback on my book. Her philosophy has convinced me that youth today are visionaries and remain the drumbeat of the future.

A special thanks to my globe-trotting comrade Mary Ann Froley. Her travel knowledge made global journeys an invaluable joy and mind-expanding experience.

I gratefully add Jo-Anne Wolfard, an English instructor and close friend who was the first to review my book early on. Under her expert scrutiny, she led me in creative directions of storytelling—and for that, my deepest thanks, Jo-Anne.

Throughout the writing of this book, my incomparable friend and confidante Linda Kemmerley, whose enthusiasm and humor was essential by her insistent mercies *to take a break,* thankfully energized me every step of the way.

I would also like to mention a cultural icon, William Edelen. A compassionate humanist and gentle kindred spirit, his symposiums in Palm Springs have enriched my sense of wonder and mystical guidance based on his book *Toward the Mystery of Being.*

In many ways I want to acknowledge my appreciation to people who willingly assisted and gave unselfishly of their time. My outreach to UCSB was greeted with enthusiasm and positive responses from Tessa Mendez, campus policy coordinator, and Carol Cox, associate director of the UCSB book store. They were a pleasure to work with and made my task a joy. I must point out the same applies to Jessie Brumfiel, director of communications, Dunn School in Los Olivos, and her colleague Sherrie Petersen, communications coordinator, for her incomparable support.

The staff at the Book Loft in Solvang, California, gave me amazing encouragement, especially Tom Gerald, for his wisdom and friendship.

Author Doug Ford was a valuable source of information and guidance through the network of publishing. Thank you, Doug, for keeping me updated.

My search for a cartographer led to World Map Source in Santa Barbara, California. Mark Walker, with his wife, Jan Ziegler, a graphic designer, proved a remarkable team of accurate artistic talent in map design production.

I must ultimately acknowledge my three siblings, who are the soul of this story. With divine reflection, by recalling and expressing our memorable and tragic experiences together as children, today my brother, Richard, and I share an unspoken bond in loving memory of Jeanne, our sister, and little brother, David. This episode in our lives has shaped and influenced me through the years in the most gratifying and profound ways.

A Very Special Thanks to Melanie Sundstrom

Melanie is a beautiful, strong, gifted woman whose training and expertise equipped her to fill the major role in supervising the manuscript. She is also a friend, comrade, and companion through all the preparation. It's hard for me to even begin describing her contribution to this work. I was once asked about our collaboration, and my answer was something to the effect that when she learned I was writing in longhand, she answered, "Oh, I can do that for you on my computer!" Thus began the long uphill journey of rewrites and corrections. Melanie was the power engine who drove the process forward—for without her this would have been a very different book, or possibly not at all! Melanie saw this story in startling new ways, and I learned a tremendous amount from just talking to her. It was providence that I met her when I needed her most.

Thank you, Mel, my friend.

About The Author

Lydia Edwards, a graduate of Antioch University in psychology and communications, has traveled to Near-East nations and Africa. A political and social activist for human rights, she co-founded the Santa Barbara County Commission for Status of Women and was appointed NGO representative to World Conference UN Decade for Women in Nairobi, Kenya. Lydia is a media contributor for regional and state-wide political, civic, and human rights awareness. She has a son and daughter and lives with her husband in California.

CPSIA information can be obtained at www.ICGtesting.com
Printed in the USA
BVOW04*1554020615

402638BV00001B/1/P

9 781480 816824